HIGH WATER

YOUNG MAN LINCOLN TRILOGY VOLUME TWO

HIGH WATER

Abraham Lincoln from the Family Farm to New Orleans, 1831

by Wayne Soini

High Water
Abraham Lincoln and his flatboat trip to New Orleans
Young Man Lincoln Trilogy Volume Two

Copyright © 2016 by Wayne Soini

Contents

Author's Introduction Print Edition

A story of bold courage is in your hands.

Be at Abraham Lincoln's side as he steps outside of his family's cabin on March 1st, 1831. Having sheltered from a terrible winter, he was intent now upon going south. His loping steps on that rainy day form but the beginning of a long, dangerous journey to New Orleans, first by dugout canoe and then by home-made flatboat, braving all of the risks that the Mississippi in flood can offer. The associations Abraham makes and the sights that Abraham sees that spring will change his life and our history to this day.

If you like this book, you'll want to join my advance-discount notification list to buy the next book in the series. You can find the link at my website, www.waynesoini.com.

If you're on my list, you'll get the chance to buy my future work at the lowest price two weeks before publication. Meanwhile, thanks for buying this first volume.

–*Wayne Soini*

CHAPTER ONE

On the first day of March, Abraham tossed off his blanket and, bypassing boots he had to save for his trip, loped swiftly and noiselessly in his stockings to the cabin's door.

For weeks, people had been praying for the snow to stop. During the chilly but windless final days of February each morning they opened their cabin doors to a heart-stopping ghostliness. The swirling gave them a start until they realized: it was not snow. A damp fog haunted them now. By high noon the sun was a faint light burning as though through a linen sheet. It warmed them, almost. Before dark, low clouds formed and swathed the prairie again, a new, thick blanket of fog. But, under that blanket, the earth warmed. The second night of it, Abraham heard river ice boom and cracks like gunshots that continued through the next day. After the third night, the snow level was down over a foot, two feet in some places. By the third afternoon, an eerie hiss rose. Winter, loth to pass, was in its death rattle. Abraham had barely slept.

At the door, he saw mist — only in his imagination.

Today was not beginning with fog. It was warm outside, warmer than it was inside the cabin. Furrowing his brow and grinning, he left the cabin door open. He waited to hear Ma.

After a minute, Ma asked, "Did you close the door, son?"

Questions were Ma's way to command.

"No, ma'am," Abraham said.

Ma was puzzled but only for a second. Then she, too, got up out of bed and went to view the road and the woods. The sun was rising clear and warm this morning.

The others in the cabin talked now, too. Winter mornings had been silent, mostly. Today it was as if their tongues were thawing and they could speak again.

Within another hour, steam rose high over banks of snow, dribbling, drooling, spilling snowbanks and, in thousands of folds and wrinkles, shrinking, collapsing began in real earnest. Drops of water formed and fell from icicles. As Abraham moved back and forth to the door, an anxious cat between the milk bowl and the sound of a mouse, he stood in the doorway, listening as drips became drip-drips, then drip-drip-drips all around the cabin, splashing into a series of puddles. What had been a trickle became a torrent.

The noises were much louder today, of ice cracking with audible pops and more booms. The river was moving. An ice jam was being forced. It was as if some great machine were going into operation. In a way, a great machine was, a winter-destroying and snow-melting machine.

Then the Heavens opened. From a distance they could hear a full-throated chorus *a–ga-KA, a–ga-KA, a–ga-KA.* Abraham took off his stockings and walked out, barefoot, to look up.

Tiny at first, but larger and larger, then overhead, came the geese. The ongoing cacophony of several wedges of geese continued as hundreds, maybe thousands, of them evidenced their abandonment of the south.

These honking birds were heading north. *North.*

What did they know?

One thing, Abraham was sure that geese enjoyed a broader view of the country than he did. What the geese knew was comforting. If geese took to their wings, it was as if a host of angels flew, singing an ode to spring.

Beside him, Abraham was joined at the front of the house by Ma and Tildy, then Pa and Johnny. They peeped at one another, sharing with raised eyebrows, tight grins and quick winks, that something was different. Each face felt the same surprise gift: warmth. It was not their imagination, it was a candle's worth without any candle, a mother's hand of gentle caress, but in such contrast to that harsh, cold, constant wind as to make them shiver at the feel of a touch of the divine. Nature was at their door as a friend and not an enemy.

Warmth.

Not bucketfuls, not hardly thimbles full, mere droplets of warmth, really, but warmth nevertheless, palpable warmth, as cunning as the cat jumping up on the bed, a surprise companion most welcome in a dark hour.

Warmth was accumulating, gathering toward a mass melt of the great snow drifts and snow banks and snow piles. That frozen kingdom was marked to collapse and fall down to nothing, to nothing at all.

Everybody suddenly talked all at once.

Tildy was gabbling on and on about nothing but geese.

Ma, quite as much taken, said three words over and over, *Listen to them.*

Pa, mute, pointed at the snow.

Johnny had a question for Abraham.

"Time?" Johnny asked, looking up at him.

Then they all felt the first patter of drops of rain.

CHAPTER TWO

On that morning of March the first the rain was not cold. It made them feel fresh, as if being bathed, a forgotten luxury. Not only that, these waters commanded that the snows melt and join in a great pell-mell rush downhill to fill rivers and ponds.

They had best be off.

"Time," Abraham said to Johnny.

"How we going?" Johnny asked.

"Hanks must say how. Maybe water roads, like over in Venice."

Johnny said nothing. *What was Venice?*

By contract with Denton Offutt, Johnny and Abraham were to meet Offutt in Springfield once the snow had "gone off." True, it had only just started to melt. True, it could start to snow again. True, they could be caught in a spring storm, even a blizzard. Snow had not yet gone off. There were not even bare spots. But that was lawyer talk. Abraham listened to the geese, and to the steady dripping and the puddles around the cabin. He decided that they had to go to Springfield.

Rain on the roof and sounds of water filled their ears. Rushing through melting snow, water would seek its level, every gully would be a sudden torrent, dry creek beds would be awash and then spill up over upper banks, high water marks that had lasted a century might be topped.

There had been so much snow. Boundaries would erase without anything to hold these waters back. Water swirled and what had been the long conversation about cold and snow and winter in home after home – and around the stove in Posey's store – turned very quickly into a panicky dialogue about rain. What had been said of snow was said of rain: how much would there be? when would it stop? did you ever see the like? God help us.

It was as if the prairie people, all farming folk, were being mocked with warmth coupled with an inability to reach their rich soil at the same time. The Deep Snow had lasted just over sixty days. Would it rain now for two months?

Misery in rain and flood was only a little less than in snow. Many despaired of ever enjoying again what they had found in such comic and constant profusion last year: a series of perfectly sunny, blue sky days. The most pious declared that they had not thanked God as He deserved and were being punished for ingratitude.

Abraham had no time to debate the weather and Johnny had no interest.

In a hasty hour, Abraham and Johnny dressed for rain and ate a last breakfast before their trip. Abraham was glad for preserving his boots dry. He had also improved an hour by splitting, shaving, filing and nailing crudely cross-hatched wood blocks for heels that would defy slippage even on ice. Pa felt them and said he ought to get a patent. It made Abraham startle: did the old man know he wanted to invent things?

After breakfast, such as it was, biscuits and gravy, and a few moments hugging and kissing Ma and Tildy, and getting back slaps and handshakes and "Wish you well, come back safe" from Pa, the two were off.

It happened fast.

Abraham and Johnny moved through wooded roads for miles, passing and greeting wary-eyed, snow-stunned, tired farmers, their wives and children, even young ones wizened and bowed down, too covered up. Faith was scarce. With so much snow in sight, so many false hopes all winter long, spring was a hope, even with geese vouching for its imminence and the warmth in the Heavens as a sign. If it was spring, where was the sun?

For miles in pouring rain, through slush, snow and mud, Abraham and Johnny moved along, Abraham always ahead, Johnny always behind, complaining and hauling his low-topped brogans up from the sucking mud. Abraham turned, his hands on his hips and asked Johnny over and over if he wanted to go back and wait until the mud dried. Johnny, of course, said no as loudly as he had been complaining. Abraham finally turned one last time and they proceeded without further complaining, turning or stopping to talk at all.

Children were out, more than adults. Faces of such children as they passed were muddy. Wearing the earth, the humus of humanity stood revealed. Clearly, it was sun that the humble needed, not mud. What could be sown or raised in mud? Would there be no crops after the terrible winter? To survive the folks here needed sun, to thrive, they needed lots of sun. Yet, wherever there was not water, there was mud. Deep, squishy, sludgy, dirty mud, mud of clay, mud mixed with gravel like raisin pudding, yellow mud, green mud, oozing mud, mud on sills, on floors, on clothes.

Above Abraham and Johnny, the skies rumbled, clouds turned slowly, wringing themselves out over a soaked prairie. Rain or no rain, Abraham trudged forward, Johnny tagging along at his heels. Blue sky today would be a miracle.

To walk or go by water for their rendezvous with Denton Offutt would be up to John Hanks. To make their way to Springfield by water would mean time to make a raft. And rafting in rushing current would not be easy. Pa had lost half the family's goods once, tossed overboard when his raft tipped across the usually placid Ohio. In swirling high water, they could lose their lives. It might be best to hoof it to Springfield.

CHAPTER THREE

Abraham wore grey-brown homespun under a roundabout coat that, when he bent to rest his burden, exposed several inches of Posey's strongest pantaloon suspenders. His large wooden-heeled cowhide boots came up under the knees of his blue jeans. An old black slouch wool hat topped his head.

Johnny wore a blue-dyed buttoned rough-cut wool shirt. Below, he was clad in Pa's old trousers. He was hoping to grow into them by the time they reached New Orleans. His trouser bottoms were rolled to hit the ankle rather than the ground, his laborer's brogans would have clomped loudly but the ground everywhere gave way, soft and muddy.

"How we going to get to Springfield?" Johnny asked.

Johnny put the question again that Abraham had been thinking about since dawn, since the rush of water and, now, rain made a good question.

More specific this time, "A raft maybe," Abraham told him.

It was as good an answer as any.

After another hour, the two stood in the rain, drenched, in front of Hanks's cabin. They hollered and pressed on the door. As they expected, they found Hanks inside, along with Susan.

Was it time to start for Offutt? Yes, Hanks agreed, they might start out.

Hanks said, "I was thinking of waiting until the rain stopped, but it might not stop."

It had stopped snowing, though — and that was sufficient. Hanks was done with doubts.

"I know of a canoe," was all he said besides.

So that was the answer.

A canoe.

There followed the usual uproar associated with possessions whenever they are wanted. When wanted for packing up, everything always seems to have legs and to skitter. Nothing is where one last saw it or expected it to be. As Hanks packed, Abraham and Johnny stripped their shirts, set before the amazing roaring fire to dry, and washed their faces and hands in the same basin, smearing a towel in the process of their cleaning, Abraham first by seniority, followed by Johnny, his junior by a year, who remained somewhat smudged.

After filling up on squirrel pie and a broth, probably of the same animal, and one potato each, Susan force-fed them flapjacks, honey with pork rind and turnip greens. It seemed to Abraham a royal send-off.

Following a tearful farewell during which Susan kissed and hugged and bid Hanks a good trip and hugged each of the boys, she prayed aloud to God that they'd all come back just fine. They opened the door to find — the rain had stopped and the sun was out with a rainbow.

Miracles did happen.

"Good sign," Abraham said.

He stood back for Hanks to go out the door first as their leader, then Johnny out of courtesy, and last himself.

Susan stood in the doorway, tears flowing more freely than rain, as off the three went.

Hanks told them that the canoe was "down the road apiece." Hanks kept his ears open. Hanks tapped neighbors as others did maple trees for sap in spring, here, there and everywhere for information. Making do with nods and pauses and minimal gestures, never needing to speak long or ask a lot of questions, he got what he needed and could use. Hanks had some time earlier found out where he might find a boat.

After a good hour, Hanks pointed.

"The canoe's up there, over by the barn," he said.

So it was, a large one. It would do for the three of them. It could have held five or six good-sized men. Where else were they going to get anything to see them downriver to Springfield?

As they skirted the cabin and wove their way through a thick stand of trees that hid a river behind, in the direction of the canoe, seemingly quiet, the resident farmer came out of his cabin carrying his shotgun and moving at a lope.

CHAPTER FOUR

"I help you?" the pioneer shouted.

On his property, the three men stopped and stood at rest, hands out, palms in sight, with sacks at their feet. Not fifty yards ahead, next to one of the trees, the farmer's large Indian-style cottonwood canoe was visible. His property.

"We were admiring your canoe, sir," Hanks said.

Hanks's hands were in his pockets, none of the three making a move, always wisest when a stranger is running around with a shotgun handy in your general vicinity.

Without suggesting that they may have had an idea of stealing his canoe that they admittedly admired, the pioneer edged into talk.

"It's a wet spring," he said.

"It is," Hanks said. "Been a cold winter."

"And a snowy one," the man said.

"We're looking for a way to get to Springfield," Hanks said.

The man nodded.

"May be too big for three. See how wide it is, and long."

"Brother, you floated it yet? For leaks?" Hanks asked.

"Yep, dry as bone. Made for me by an Indian last summer. I told him a cottonwood canoe and he felled a twenty-foot tree across the river, burned it, hollowed it out and carved away with an ax. Didn't take him two weeks. Name's Slater, Erastus Slater. Yours?"

Beginning with John Hanks, they all gave their names.

"How much you pay the Indian?" Hanks asked.

"Didn't. We bartered for some jugs."

The Indian was paid in corn liquor, not even blankets.

Hanks asked, "You interested in selling?"

"You interested in buying, Hanks?"

"It'd be a mite big but it could do."

Slater said. "Make me an offer."

With that, he put the shotgun down to his side. He continued holding it, though, at the ready.

"You in the militia?" Hanks asked, thinking it likely.

"I am. You?"

"I am in the Spies," Hanks said, the Spies being the non-uniformed scouts.

11

"Well, I guess there'd be no harm in me making a brotherly offer of selling this canoe for...ten dollars."

"We are only going to use it one time, to get from here to Springfield, Captain," Hanks said, granting Slater a complimentary rank. "Probably have to sell it cheap when we get there. We are going to New Orleans."

"Canoes be in demand, Hanks. But I say, for you, my friend, ten's fair," Slater said.

"We're getting ten dollar gold pieces, bonuses in New Orleans," Johnny said.

Hanks gave Johnny a stare. Abraham stepped his boot on Johnston's brogan. *Enough.*

Slater smiled.

"What were you thinking, Hanks?"

"Six-fifty, specie, Erastus. It's been a hard winter."

"Well, we do got that winter in common."

"And militia," Hanks said.

The agreed on seven-fifty, with oars, and Slater threw in a tarp.

"Fair deal," Johnny said.

"No thanks to you," Hanks said as Slater was gone to fetch the oars and tarp.

"Worked out. Got oars we thought we'd have to cut and carve," Abraham said.

Hanks said, "Johnny, help Erastus with the oars and tarp. Make us proud, will you?"

Hanks traded a look with Abraham, who smiled. Hanks was a shrewd one. To make peace, allow the sinner his penance.

CHAPTER FIVE

Then they were on the river.

Billows of river fog masked any progress. By logic, they were drifting in the right direction, but that was logic. It appeared that they were floating without any aim in acres of clouds, in and out of visibility and obscurity, being and not being, on earth and outside of it. Landless water, no matter how shallow, without a visible shore, seals a body off from the rest of the universe. The audible sound of rushing water near shore dissipated and, by midstream, muted to the point of vanishing. In the silence they could hear their own heartbeats. After months in a small cabin where every sound, creak of timber, crackle in fire, a distant wolf's howl was always amplified, the great quiet around them was eerie. Where had everybody gone? Had the wild critters died in the winter? If they were alive, had they not heard the call of the geese? Travel on this river was not as on horseback clip-clopping, dogs barking, or birds singing.

At a bend in the river, willow trees appeared in battle. Bent and bowing to assaults of the tugging, overpowering water, their yellow light green reflecting the primeval battle between land and water, unwilling to be pulled under.

The men in the canoe continued drifting and rowing to keep steady in the rushing water. As mist lifted and sunshine came striking through, mirrors suddenly appeared everywhere. Objects and reflections were indistinguishable, inseparable. The trees doubled in height by the magic of reflections.

They were making more progress faster than they could reckon. The current helped draw them along while they rowed, too. So much around them was the same for the first two hours that the illusion of circling around the same area of the same river was impossible to shake, illusion though it was.

"This flood'll drown the snakes and rabbits," Johnny said.

"Some always survive. Like us," Hanks said.

Abraham said, "We're like Noah."

"No," Hanks said. "Noah didn't have to worry about meeting up with Denton Offutt. He only had to float and wait for the water to go down."

Abraham was happy enough to sing and started a ditty about a farmer's daughter who possessed a boil in a peculiar place when the canoe scraped and struck something solid. The three all but fell into the flood.

"Might be a rock," Johnny said.

"Might be top of a church steeple," Hanks said, unusually talkative, excited even, "Johnny, see if you can use the oar as a pole, it's easiest on your side."

Johnny did probe a bit, quite attentively. Abraham pulled a prank, shouting and scared him, which led him to swing his oar about as if to strike Abraham, who blocked the oar and, grabbing it in both hands, twisted it and hiked Johnny up and over the side of the canoe into the water with a splash.

"Stop it. Fish him out, Abe."

Abraham, who caught the flash in Hanks's eyes and grew silent, with care to balance properly, made a swift and skillful move with his hands for Johnny to grab ahold of him which, once done by floundering, water-spluttering Johnston, allowed Abraham to gently haul Johnny up out of the water and back aboard.

"Did you touch bottom?" Abraham asked.

"I'll touch your bottom," Johnny said, coughing.

"You swung the oar, John, but I forgive you," Abraham said.

"You forgive me? Oh, that's a good one."

Johnny crossed his arms, pouting and shivering.

"Johnny, have no hard feelings. Abraham apologized," Hanks said.

"He did not," Johnny said.

"Abraham?"

"I'm sorry, Johnny, for defending myself against you reaching to strike me with that oar of yours."

"Abraham," Hanks said, gruffly now, though covering a laugh with a cough.

"Okay, I am sorry. Truly, I wish and beg for you to forgive me, cousin," Abraham said.

"It going to happen again?" Johnny asked.

"I'll never throw you off the canoe again, cousin, my word of honor," Abraham promised, raising his right hand.

"Done and done," Hanks said. "We got to make time to beat the dark. We can't tell where we are exactly, very likely not in the river channel, maybe making circles over and over in a cornfield."

CHAPTER SIX

Hanks kept saying how anything that can't swim is drowning and wondering how far north you would have to go before anybody was planting potatoes. Abraham guessed Canada.

It misted up again into a tick, cool, prickly-dropped fog. How thick the fog was hereabouts, it blinded them from seeing how much the river had risen as well as where they were. It was almost scary how alone they were, or at least felt. Were they to spill now, would they find one another, and the canoe? Were they far from shore? And from any help?

The river was in flood and rising. Doubtless, downstream water was spilling even more over old banks and covering anything flat, which was most all of central Illinois. Which farmer was safe? All who had survived winter faced a new enemy, growing strong by absorbing the strength of the old one. This was the spring incarnation of the Deep Snow, now become the Big Melt.

Abraham hooted, "Hallo!"

It echoed but there was no other answer.

"What are you doing?" Johnny asked.

"I'm trying to see if anybody else is around and just where they think they are, if there's anybody."

"We seem alone," Hanks said.

Abraham said, "Alone together."

Hanks said to Abraham, "Yeah. You be Noah and I'll be Columbus, but what does that make John D. Johnston?"

"That makes him...poor old John," Abraham said, tickling Johnny and laughing.

"Watch your hat," Hanks said, seeing Johnny reach up, grab and toss Abraham's hat out onto the flood.

Abraham began to go for Johnny, who defended himself by saying, "You promised, you gave your word, you wouldn't throw me in the water again."

Abraham started rocking the canoe with his feet, back and forth, making Johnny slide on the seat of the canoe, then roll forward and almost pitch out.

"That's enough, I'll get the hat, you two stop your nonsense," Hanks said, navigating the canoe back and around with quick strokes.

"Stop your nonsense," Johnny said.

"Poor Johnny," Abraham said.

"You — Noah," Johnny said.

"Well, Johnny, if you call the tail of a sheep a leg, how many legs has a sheep?" Abraham asked.

"Five," Johnny said.

"No, only four," Abraham said.

"Yeah, but you said to call a tail a leg," Johnny said.

"Now, Johnny, does calling a tail a leg make it a leg?"

Hanks roared with laughter as he reached for the hat and, snagging it on the end of his oar, tossed it over to Abraham.

"Good one, Abe, never heard that one. You just think it?" Hanks asked.

"No, I read it somewhere. Wait, I hear something," Abraham said, pointing.

It was faint but a dog was barking.

Hanks said, "You're right. Let's get to rowing. Maybe a farm or something."

They started rowing in earnest, only Johnny smoldering, hot over being played for the ignoramus, the rube, when he talked smoother than Abraham could except for hard words and facts that did not mean anything.

That dog was really bellowing now.

CHAPTER SEVEN

The poor dog was in the river, swimming — or drowning.

"Hey, boy," Abraham said in a calm tone, reaching over the edge of the canoe and taking him up and out of the water.

It was soaked, of course, and shook itself. Tired or not, the dog was all excited and kept leaping up at Abraham and licking him, making whimpering sounds all the while.

"Whose dog is it?" Johnny asked.

"Look at him, he's telling us who," Hanks said.

"Cousin, do we need a dog going down the Mississippi?" Johnny asked.

Hanks shook his head and said, "Can't say I ever needed one."

But Hanks was smiling, watching the dog and its new master.

"I'm going to name him Tiger, he's got tiger eyes. They burn bright," Abraham said.

Johnny said, "He's going to be no use, Abraham. I say dump him."

Abraham was holding its head in both hands and talking soothingly.

Then Abraham looked up and said to Johnny, "I'll dump you."

"Just you try," he said, taking his oar up out of the water and moving it out straight like a spear in Abraham's direction.

"Keep rowing, Johnny," Hanks told him.

After a minute's tension, Johnny commenced to rowing again.

Johnny said, "Stupid dog. Don't have a use for dogs on boats."

"Can't let him drown," Abraham said.

Hanks said, "No, but it might be we can find someone to keep him. The flatboat's no place for a dog."

"Or maybe we can eat him," Johnny said, laughing.

Abraham looked up at Johnny, his hands off the dog and in the air as he made a leap toward and upon Johnny.

"You said you wouldn't toss me," Johnny said.

"Ain't going to," Abraham said, "alive."

"Abraham," Hanks said.

The dog was barking now.

"Listen to Tiger bark," Hanks said.

Abraham let go of Johnny and sat back with the dog. It was not clear why but the dog was licking Abraham's face, and Abraham was silent as they drifted on downriver.

17

CHAPTER EIGHT

Abraham was a free man whose hands were his wealth. He could chop trees or shoe horses. He could claim a farm, as his father had several times. Meanwhile, he could row a canoe.

Pa was planning his same old plan. Once they steamed back up from New Orleans, Pa was going to sell the farm. Then they would go back to Indiana the way they came and on the same wagons, different oxen. Everyone had voted yes.

He looked at Johnny and wondered what the boy thought, if he ever did. Abraham was not going to stay in Illinois, to hire out, removing rocks and stumps, splitting rails, setting fences, plowing again. In Indiana, he would claim his own little farm and invent. He'd set up a blacksmith shop to fund his invention factory. He'd work out how to make guns, plows and predict weather, sow corn and harvest it better than now. He'd develop river inventions, governors on steam boilers and buoyant chambers. He had lots of thoughts all the time. He thought about the waters under them.

The three of them, Abraham, his younger step brother and his older cousin, rode upon the Deep Snow, melted. The huge and constant fall from out of the sky in December and January and for so much of February, that snow, along with the freezing rain that had turned instantly to ice, was now so much water that overflowed banks, water that would take them to New Orleans. All of this water, every drop, was heading to New Orleans, to the sea. The Deep Snow was under them now, the whited sepulcher melted into so much water. The blizzards that once struck to snuff life out were gone, and in place, under them, a living, flowing, life-sustaining servant.

The dark forests beside them, the sunlit high patches of barely-leaved birches, were doubled by upside-down reflections in the waters. Nothing stood alone or upward by itself but it simultaneously thrust its twin down into the earth, an illusion on the thin surface of the water seeming every bit as substantial as the real. Only the mind could separate the real from the illusory.

Johnny spoke.

"Is this like going down the Mississippi?" Johnny asked.

It was clear to whom Johnny was talking, and to whom he was not talking.

Hanks said, "No, it's spring flood. There's no shoal water here, nothing very shallow. The river, the Mississippi, is very much wider, you can't see the shores usually, both at once."

"That big?" Johnny asked.

"That big and that long, and slower, except for rapids," Hanks said.

"What do we do in rapids?"

"You'll find out. Best travel in the middle mostly, keep away from banks. But rocks and bars and logs, you watch out for them, too."

"Many of them, cousin?" Johnny asked.

"Plenty. We are traveling easier here, and much faster than our flatboat will ever go."

With that, Hanks "wa-hooed" and dug his oar into the water as if to surge forward even faster.

"See our wake?" Hanks asked Johnny.

"It is kind of foamy," Johnny said, looking and giving the bubbles behind them more dignity than they deserved.

For the first time, Abraham smiled. He was thinking of his trip with Allen Gentry. He had learned a host, a legion of words, improved his vocabulary by associating himself with Gentry. The river had been his classroom. Here Johnny was wasting time on bubbles and foam.

Hanks had not even mentioned the steamboats, steamboats that, piloted indifferently, could come up and collide with roll over a flatboat, leaving no one to tell the tale. Flatboats, by accident, would run into steamboats. Johnston had no idea.

Abraham exulted in feeling free. It was so different to be in a canoe on rushing water under the open sky than to be in a cabin with the folks. Abraham had awakened all his life in cabins, but he had never felt so awake, so alert, so interested as when on the water. It was like being reborn.

Abraham left off with the dog, who rested. He picked up an oar just as Hanks had an instruction.

Hanks told Abraham, "Watch the log. Your side."

Abraham saw it coming only after Hanks's warning, and raised his oar to let it pass. Hanks said nothing more. They all rowed without much concern, the current carrying them. Before day's end, their canoe came in at the landing of Judy's Ferry. No problem sliding up today, the waterline was lapping right up to the boathouse with its large sign "Boats."

From that boathouse, Hanks knew where they were. Some five miles east of Springfield. They did not spot Offutt nor expect to spot him in among the three loungers sitting at a bench inside, whittling and drinking. Two of them ran the ferry but the ferry was not running. They had pulled their lines in and were hunkered down to wait further developments. One was Uriah Mann.

Hanks knew Mann. Hanks stood in the canoe, quite an acrobatic move but he was agile, and shouted through cupped hands, "Ho, Mann."

"Ho, who?" Mann shouted back. "Who you?"

The loungers laughed.

"Hanks," he said.

"Oh, I remember you now," Mann said. They were both in the militia.

The canoe came up to the ramp and steps now, and Hanks took rope and tied while Abraham stowed the oars and soothed Tiger and Johnny gawked.

Unnecessarily, Mann jerked a thumb at the kingdom behind him and said that it was his boat-house and storage. He finished by asking if he could be of service. Hanks introduced his two relatives, and asked Mann if he had seen Denton Offutt.

CHAPTER NINE

"Offutt? You know Offutt?" Mann asked, smiling as if the name kindled a fond or entertaining memory.

"Offutt," Hanks said.

"Yes, Offutt has been around more times than I can count, trying to find a flatboat," Mann said.

"And any number of times to buy the ferry," one of the ferrymen said, chuckling.

"But not for cash," the other ferryman said, chuckling more.

"Promissory notes," the original ferryman said, not chuckling, his mouth mashing as if tasting something sour.

Mann told Hanks, "The fact is, boats are in short supply, flatboats especially. You see why. Water, water everywheres."

Hanks explained they had just come down from Macon County by canoe, which they would like to store. Hanks saw the likelihood of Offutt being ready to head off to New Orleans in a flatboat was remote. Best to keep a canoe at the ready to go back up on home. Mann was in charge and nodded fine.

"At your own risk if we get flooded," Mann said.

He was not the owner. The true owners of the boathouse and landing were a Springfield merchant, Elijah Iles, in partnership with land speculator Peter Van Bergen. Mann scheduled the ferry and undertook to hold and store and to repair boats. His main carpenter, John E. Rolls, was away in Springfield.

"Some folks are paying big for fencing against the flood, and boarding places up fast. Rolls'll make a buck either way, rain or shine."

"We're looking for Offutt," Johnny said, impatient with all this talk.

"Try and hire you, he will," Mann said.

"Already hired," Johnny said, which got the ferrymen both to laughing and snorting.

"What's so funny?" Johnny asked. "I got a contract."

Abraham placed a hand upon Johnny's shoulder, easing him.

"He got a contract," one ferryman said.

"With Offutt," the other said, slamming down a fist and laughing.

"Johnny," Abraham said, softly, "we got business."

Hanks dealt with the practical matter of having the canoe here and ready if they needed it. For the cost of one dollar, at their own risk in case of flood, Mann would stow their canoe up inside the barn-like building.

Hanks, angling toward a better deal, said, "How about if we are not back in a week, you sell it? Canoe like this has value."

"Maybe, maybe not. I'll give you back your dollar and four more, total five. How's that?"

"Fair," Hanks said.

Hanks either had the canoe they needed or, after a week, five dollars on his next pass-through. They shook hands and Hanks passed Mann a silver dollar.

Spotting no wagons headed in the thick mud to Springfield, after washing up at the pump, the day being fair and the canoe stowed (and likely soon sold), the three men began to hoof it to town, the dog walking smartly at Abraham's heels.

CHAPTER TEN

They found Offutt. It was easier than they thought.

Hanks simply approached a passing pair of farmers, seemingly a father and son, and asked, "Do you know Denton Offutt?"

That question netted Hanks a laugh.

"Is he a gassy, windy, rattle-brained talker?"

That was the older man.

The younger said, "He'll try and talk you into selling your coat for his buttons."

"He does talk, we know," Hanks said.

"Try and hire you, he will," the younger said.

The older one shook his head as if to warn: *don't do it.*

This time, Johnny said nothing about the contract or being hired already.

"You know where Offutt is at?" Hanks asked.

"Try the Buckhorn," the young one said, smirking and netting himself a laugh from the old man before they proceeded.

"You know where the Buckhorn is?" Abraham asked Hanks in an undertone.

"I do," Hanks said, his face set and solemn. He was walking forward in long, stiff strides, leaving Abraham and Johnny to keep up despite the sacks they were hauling.

Following Hanks, they went wordlessly past fields, a stand of oak and maple, three houses under construction, a church and a store, a couple small houses, one with a sign "Shoes" on its door, until they came to a two-story largish building, like an inn, with a signboard hanging from a rod without words but a crude painting of a buck's head.

Inside the Buckhorn, bartender and innkeeper Andrew Elliott, a taciturn man with a banged-up, bandaged head, responded to Hanks's inquiry. Elliott gestured with a nod of his head and a bent index finger stroke of his nose.

Following with their eyes, they all saw Offutt at once, a figure asleep or at least prone and motionless atop a table at the rear of the establishment.

Lincoln asked, "The dog all right?"

Andrew asked in turn, "Why? he got worms?"

Abraham said no.

Andrew nodded and wiped the counter.

25

Given the late hour of the day, they felt permitted without discourtesy to awaken Offutt and, Hanks leading, proceeded in file.

Up at the wooden altar on which Offutt lay as if to be sacrificed, Hanks scuffed the floor and ahemed, which got Johnny to laughing although Hanks was not intending humor.

They noted that the man stirred.

Dreamy Offutt opened his eyes to find three angels standing around him.

"Saint Peter?" Offutt asked Hanks.

"Guess again. You told us to come down here after the snow melted. The snow melted and, like the clown says at the start of the circus, here we are."

"Where — how'd you get here so fast?" Offutt asked, sitting up and rubbing his eyes. His head felt sore and swollen.

"By canoe down the Sangamon and meadows flooded around and about it. Landed at Judy's Ferry," Hanks said.

Offutt squeezed his eyes closed, thinking over the buzz in his head. Judy's Ferry. He remembered bits of fact now.

"That's five miles," Offutt said.

Hanks, chin high and raising his right foot, slapped the top of his thigh, saying, "Shank's mare."

"Let me up," Offutt said, although nobody was opposing him, as he struggled at first to stand and then fell back onto the bench.

Seated thus, Offutt called to the tavern's owner, "Andrew, a round for my friends and me, if you please, sir."

When Offutt saw Tiger, he added, "And a dish of your best water, please, for this fine canine specimen."

"Offutt, you got your two men yet?" Hanks asked.

His head hanging low and staring at the floor, Offutt said, "That arrangement has fallen through. Sorrowfully, I have clasped hands with several who promised but have not kept not their word."

"We had your word," Hanks said.

"Why, so you did and so you have, Brother — Hanks, was it not?"

"Hanks it was and is, with me my cousin, Abraham Lincoln, and Johnny Johnston, who signed contracts, too."

"Ah, Wisconsin."

"You keep saying that," Johnny said. "I ain't never been to Wisconsin."

"You'd like it," Offutt said.

"The flatboat?" Hanks asked.

"That is, as I mentioned in your rustic and quaintly-appointed abode, my responsibility entirely."

Offutt recounted dramatically how he had been scouting everywhere in vain for a flatboat to buy or to rent, or to hear word of somebody somewhere who might have a flatboat to sell or to rent.

"Some were lost in the flood. Not mine, though. Luckily, I had no flatboat to lose. Can you imagine the tragedy avoided? Nothing wrecked, as it is. My fortunes are *intactus*."

"In Texas?" Johnny asked.

"*Intactus*, Latin for untouched."

Offutt, waving at the bartender, who was arriving with drinks and a dish of water, said to Hanks, "Ask my good friend, Andrew, over there. The builders of boats have lost their cradles and yards around here. And lumber, you know – wood floats. That's the story. We are downstream of a big flood – a flood that only grows bigger every day."

Abraham took the water dish and placed it down in front of Tiger. The dog looked up as if to ask, "Did you think I was thirsty? Do you not understand that I am hungry?"

"Buy a ferry," Hanks told Offutt.

"I tried. They want cash money."

Hanks was not happy but, knowing what he had heard at the ferry, he was pleased that Offutt was honest with them. Hanks was honest in return.

"We know. We were up at the ferry," Hanks said.

Abraham rose and walked off to speak with Andrew.

"You know what else?" Offutt asked.

"What else?" Hanks asked.

Offutt said, "My considered decision is that the flatboat we want is near, very near, free of charge and free-standing. It is rooted on the people's land."

"What's he mean?" Johnny asked.

Hanks frowned.

"Offutt means there are free-standing trees on Congress land that we may fell and steal, saw and split, to provide timber, to provide us with a flatboat. Of our own making."

"Can we do that?" Johnny asked.

Hanks did not answer Johnny but turned to Offutt, massaging the stubble of beard growth on his chin.

CHAPTER ELEVEN

Hanks said, "Offutt, we have left the canoe at Judy's Ferry in care of Mr. Uriah Mann with instructions that he may sell that canoe in one week if we did not return for it. He is minding the canoe meanwhile, as if it were his own. We may as well return home."

"Please," Offutt said. "Drink up and hear my plan in greater detail."

"Leave us talk on that, Mr. Offutt. But, first, me and my partners, we're going outside to talk."

Abraham gave Tiger a ham bone to occupy him while they conferred.

Once outside, Hanks told Abraham and Johnny that they could go back, of course.

"We'll be paddling upstream. Strong current. We might have to wait here before we try and go back, after the spring torrent."

They had days, maybe a week to wait.

"What's your idea?" Abraham asked Hanks.

"Let's hear him out. You know what your father always says about a bad bargain."

"Hug it the tighter," Abraham and Johnny said in chorus, smiling. As if Pa's wisdom was going to get them through this tight spot. As it turned out, it did.

The trio trotted back into the tavern, all unsmiling. Hanks picked up a glass, slowly sipped, then wiped his beard with the back of his hand and said to Offutt, "Go on."

Offutt, staring each one of them in the face in turn, said, "Gentlemen, firstly let us admit, along with the great Shakespeare, that 'the tears live in an onion that should water this sorrow.' You win. Yours is the victory over Offutt. I have no choice, no choice at all: Denton Offutt must offer you top wages and the best conditions as builders of a flatboat, better terms than any I ever offered previously to any builder."

"What terms?" Hanks asked, sitting down on the bench on the other side of the table.

"By the way, while I think of it, you must go and get that canoe from Mr. Mann," Offutt said.

"I must?" Hanks asked.

"Only — don't go back home — take it to a spot of your own wise selection

29

alongside the river, in the Congress land. You with your sharp eyes will spy a likely place to fell timber, a task that will take you one or two weeks."

"Two, at least. Besides good weather, we'll need saws and axes, awls, hammers, mauls."

"Done, done and done."

Offutt obviously had credit. Springfield merchants shared, along with Offutt, great expectations. Without many ready-money customers, to move inventory, they gave credit.

"Where is there a mill for the lumber?" Hanks asked.

"Kirkpatrick has a saw mill down at Prairie Creek, that's —"

"I know where Prairie Creek is. Will he cut our timber?"

"I know Kirkpatrick personally. He and I are old friends. Our trust in one another is as brothers."

Abraham and Johnny looked at one another. Brothers? The trust to which Offutt made reference was likely one that waxed and waned.

"Any other terms, Offutt?" Hanks said.

"Only, after the mill, rope the finished timber. Make a log raft and take it down to Sangamon Town. There stand by to assemble our river craft."

"Well, our term back is to be fed and housed."

Offutt thought, then slammed the table.

"Hot damn. While you're working in the woods, I know a widow, a good Dutch cook she is, and I'll board you with her two meals a day, morning and night. You can sleep in her barn."

"What about Sangamon Town?"

"In Sangamon Town you can make a suitably comfortable shanty until the flatboat's ready to load and launch. One of you, of course, must be cook—"

Hanks said, "Lincoln, you are elected. I can't cook an egg and I don't trust Johnny to wash his hands."

He then turned to Offutt.

"Boards and nails for the shanty. The wage terms all in coin," Hanks said.

"Fifteen dollars a month for each," Offutt said.

"Wow," Johnny said.

Hanks turned to Johnny and, a forefinger raised, said, "Shut."

He turned to Offutt and asked, "All in coin, agreed or not?"

"Coin, of course, coin – gold coin. But I would seek and anticipate, among us trusting friends, time to raise coin by selling cargo in New Orleans."

"Notes now, not coin," Hanks said, his mouth mashing now as if tasting something sour.

"Trust me. We are partners."

"Offutt, we won't need a full month to make you a boat. Give us silver or copper coin by the week."

"In coin? Well, then, three dollars per every seven days."

"Still good wages," Johnny said.

"Shut," Hanks said.

To Offutt, Hanks said, "We shall be paid no less than ten dollars in coin for three weeks' minimum even if we finish sooner."

Offutt looked down at his feet, then up to the ceiling as if for information or for patience, then said, in a resigned tone, "Gentlemen, you have poor Offutt over a barrel here. Ten dollar gold pieces for each of you upon completion of the ark that shall take us all to New Orleans."

"Give the gold pieces to the barkeep to hold."

"Certainly, Hanks, my dear friend. It will be my pleasure. Only I must call upon certain other friends of mine—"

"We'll give you 'til tomorrow. We stay tonight as your guests, do we not?"

"I had been just about to invite you at stay here at my cost, to be liberally fed, refreshed and sheltered."

"Sleep on the tables?" Johnny asked.

Offutt and Hanks discussed further details as the tavern got busy preparing for guests. All at Offutt's charge, after eating and drinking, the three were put up on the second floor in the tavern's store room, sleeping on the floor in dusty buffalo robes, robes that they quickly discovered also to be flea-ridden. Sleepless for a long while, they talked about plans for their flatboat, how big it should be, how tall the trees they would fell.

"We got a cargo of hogs to allow for," Hanks said.

"Hogs?" Johnny asked.

"Yes, and not only hogs, pork, bacon, corn and barrels, jugs. Full cargo. No matter, we shall have a good, solid flatboat to our specifications – and a mechanic's lien."

"What's that?" Johnny asked.

Abraham said, "If Offutt does not pay us, we sell the boat in this high water. We pay ourselves."

"The boat will be worth a lot," Johnny said.

"Offutt will want to pay to keep it and us," Hanks said.

"I want a room with a window," Johnny said.

"No windows," Hanks said, shaking his head.

"Why not?" Johnny asked.

"Storms. Boat needs to be tight," Hanks said.

"But won't it stink?" Johnny said.

"Nothing you ain't smelled before," Abraham said, smiling.

"I need air," Johnny said.

"Just spend more time above decks," Hanks said. "We'll want to stack the cargo right and keep ourselves back from the hogs and slop and shit."

"That's good," Johnny said.

"Glad you agree," Abraham said.

Gesturing now as if he were cutting and punching the boat together on the spot, Hanks said, "Make a way to get in back, a scuttle hole and a ladder, big steps."

"We make a mast?" Abraham asked.

Hanks shook his head.

"No canvas," Hanks said.

"Plank sails, then" Abraham said.

"Plank sails?" Hanks and Johnny both asked.

Then Hanks smiled and said, "Well, plank sails we could have."

Hanks was always of a mind to favor his ingenious cousin, who had built a tiny mill on a shoveled side of a brook back in Spencer County. It took Abraham but two weeks and worked, grinding wheat into a sort of flour. Just a bunch of found stones, timbers split, sawed, planed and pegged into place along with a cart wheel he repaired. If Abraham said he would make sails out of planks, Hanks would bet on Abraham to make sails out of planks.

"No other sails?" Johnny asked.

"Plank sails," Abraham said, saying aloud what he had never conceived existing one minute before. They did build a flatboat with planks to catch the wind.

Plank sails pleased Abraham, whose mind would not rest. Up in the second-floor storeroom of the Buckhorn that night, Abraham's tousled, bristly-haired head was dancing with ideas. Twitching and scratching under the mangy buffalo robe, Abraham was trying and imagining various designs for plank sails, grooves to slide them on, not unlike the ridges and grooves in cabinets that he and Pa had been putting together for years. They had made cabinets. Cabinets and coffins. He finally fell asleep.

CHAPTER TWELVE

The next day after eggs, bacon, toast and coffee at the tavern Hanks said that all was "on the account of Mr. Offutt" – who was still sleeping — and they made their way back to Mann to reclaim their canoe. Given Mann's lugubrious countenance, he must have counted on his contingent right of ownership. He glared as if they were stealing their craft.

"Care for tobacco, Brother Mann?" Hanks asked, offering a small bag he had brought as a present.

Mann took it without saying thanks. Militia membership only went so far.

Hanks said, "You took good care of our canoe. Thank you."

Mann remained mute.

"Well, I guess we'll be off," Hanks said. "Any message for Offutt you care to give us?"

Mann continued to glare.

Things like this amused Hanks. And Abraham. Only Johnny was puzzled and asked, "Why didn't he speak?"

Once launched, Hanks rowed right, left, right, left and was calm and disciplined, keeping his own criticisms of Offutt in check. Abraham, stalwart and straight in front, steered the canoe, propelling it firmly forward, the master of the moment. Johnny sat quietly in back, wondering when they would eat and what they would eat. Water rushed by as they cut through and along the river. Hanks declared where they were minute after minute, given the local names.

"This here is Blair's Turn, over that side is the Widow's," he said. He pointed downstream and said, "We'll go past Easton Village before we reach Congress land."

Neither Abraham nor Johnny particularly expected to be in Springfield again to find this information useful.

Along the Congress land finally, they slowed, searching for a promising place. Abraham was the first to spot a good stand of trees. Hanks agreed and aimed for it.

"*Intactus*," Johnny said. "Untouched. In Latin."

Hanks smiled and told Abraham, "The boy's learning, ain't he?"

"I'm no boy, most on to twenty-one," Johnny said.

Johnny, feeling pressed, told Abraham to get his dog back.

"Tiger's not touching you," Abraham said.

"He is all sprawl," Johnny said.

"Free country," Abraham said.

Johnny sighed.

"Not for me," he said. "For dogs."

The trees stood at the mouth of Spring Creek. Thus, the creek was good for launching and floating their fallen trees down to Kirkpatrick's mill. They stood admiring their choice. The next thing, they heard Offutt singing loudly as he approached along the shore:

> *Awake, awake, arise, all,*
> *And hail the glorious morn:*
> *Hark, how the angels sing,*
> *"To you a Saviour's born!"*

They wondered that Offutt had found them, and, seeing another figure, short but fast-moving, who was with him. Once Offutt was up to them, he bellowed "Hurrah" and introduced the man beside him as John R. Rolls.

"I met Mr. Rolls down to the Fitzpatrick sawmill, gentlemen, very highly recommended by the foreman there, Charles Broadwell, with whom I have drunk many a toast at the Buckthorn. Mr. Rolls is a carpenter by trade and profession. His skills include the building of flatboats and those he has built have all floated. Floating being the key element in a flatboat, I aim and declare that John Rolls shall have his proper role in the making of the first of the Offutt fleet. Now, boys, listen and John here will tell you how to do it."

"Boys," Johnny said, whispering.

Hanks looked at Abraham with a slight raising of his left eyebrow.

"I don't make speeches," Rolls said to his three auditors, "I don't make speeches. I work and I make pins."

Left to say something himself, Offutt said, "Let's applaud the gentleman and our project together, whether pins or needles, may it be a great success."

Offutt led the clapping, in which Abraham and Johnny joined, although Hanks only stood apart and frowned.

"You're not clapping, Hanks," Offutt said, as the applause ceased.

"Clap when it's over and we got our boat to go to New Orleans, Mr. Offutt, sir," Hanks said. He retained a tart resentment for having to build the flatboat rather than finding one, as had been promised. It had nonetheless made his side of the ledger more profitable, so he accepted it. But Rolls was a harder pill for him to swallow.

Rolls soon proved himself by hewing and scoring the timber. Hanks approved of a carpenter who stressed the importance of making measurements very carefully and followed that principle in his practice. Hanks had no desire to cut a single tree more than they had to. Rolls seemed to have a very specific idea of the dimensions of the boat. As Rolls talked, this flatboat was going to be larger than Hanks had ever been on and it dwarfed the one Abraham had built with his father and Hanks back in Indiana – which had run full eighteen feet across and almost eighty feet long. This one was going to be over eighty feet long, boxy with heavy beams, over twenty feet wide, a veritable ark. It would hold more than fifty, sixty tons of cargo. Its cabin in the stern would easily sleep four (though one or two must always be on duty above decks).

The only part Hanks did not like, although Abraham seemed to be afire with interest and Johnny's mouth was open, was the extended talking that Rolls engaged in virtually selling the boat. After talking about his design, he described "a bow that will not shatter upon collision or any other insult," and the "desirable necessity" of making their oak-shielded boat pointed at both ends.

"You got to watch out for 'sawyers,' logs that'll snag you, that float but are water-logged, and 'sleeping sawyers,' that hide just under the surface to snag you worse, by surprise, take you all down to the bottom, you don't want that, swimming around with the 'gators, gentlemen," Rolls said. He did not make speeches? Hanks looked down at the ground in order not to encourage more from Rolls about fitting their yet-to-be-built craft with oar-slots, "wooden pins of white oak," on either side, affording alternative spots for plying their oars, for more flexible navigability.

Offutt was the chorus at Rolls's side. Offutt said, "Good," and "Eminently satisfactory," and such to these suggested innovations immediately. At the end, or a pause – Hanks was unsure which — Offutt said how grateful he was for Rolls's advice.

Johnny yawned as Hanks looked sour. Abraham, standing with eyes flashing, seemed to see Rolls as an inventor and to want to be an inventor himself.

Rolls talked on. They would steer with a long sweep at the stern, he said. Rolls promised to make that key item himself, "made to order." Rolls spoke of a "caboose" in their flatboat, housing that would host a brick cook-stove "with a covered stove-pipe." That would be quite different from the campfires Abraham and Allen had had to stop and make, rain or shine, along the banks during their journey southward. He could actually appreciate that.

Once Rolls ceased to flow, Hanks spoke up.

"That will took two weeks just to cut the wood. Let us start," Hanks said.

Rolls, if he had more he could say or intended to say, stifled himself.

"You're right, Hanks," Rolls said, nodding.

Hanks, having started talking, however, kept on, saying, "And it will take more time for this Kirkpatrick's men to do the millwork. Then, I reckon, a full month after to get the hull done, flipped, and the top deck and rear room, scuttle hole, ladder, all you are talking about and top grooves for two plank sails."

"Plank sails?" Rolls asked.

"Abraham's idea," Hanks said, patting Abraham on the shoulder.

Abraham's cheeks were red and he was grinning.

Rolls took it that plank sails it was and nodded, "Fine. Then the boat must be caulked and made leak-proof with clay daubs all over, am I not correct, Hanks?"

"You are correct, sir," Hanks said with a little bow that was not mocking.

Offutt said, "I see that I stand in the presence of experienced builders before whom I need say nothing more."

"You never needed say nothing at all," Johnny said.

"Oh, I think we've all said what we should, no more, no less, Johnny. Be a patient boy, won't you?" Offutt said.

Johnny frowned, feeling anything but patience welling up inside.

Offutt added, "Now, shall we not build our shanty and then pass around a little brown jug I hold here?"

Offutt held it up.

"We don't drink," Hanks said, "but you do as you want, you and Rolls."

"I drink," Johnny said.

"You do?" Abraham asked.

"Pa said I could," Johnny said.

"Did he mean you could in New Orleans or along the way?"

"Any time."

"In Pa's absence, you are my responsibility, Johnny."

"I say I drink."

"One swig won't hurt a boy, Abe," Offutt said. He gave Abraham a wink. "I'll see to it that it stops with one swig."

"What if'n I want more?" Johnny asked Offutt.

Offutt shook his head and said, "You shan't have more, Johnnycakes, than is good for you. But a swig will, as I say, do you no harm."

"A swig then. You see, Abe? I can have a swig."

Abraham wiped his mouth with his hand in order not to expose his smile.

CHAPTER THIRTEEN

The shanty was not but three-sided and before a fire by the time the sun set. Offutt taught them all a song:

Awake, ye saints, and raise your eyes,
Rise and raise your voices high;
Awake, and praise that sovereign love
That shows salvation nigh.
Not many years their rounds shall run,
Nor many mornings rise,
Ere all its glories stand revealed
To our admiring eyes.

"This is especially fine sung full-voiced in the early morning," Offutt said, "but take heed before someone throws a shoe or curses you with sufficient seriousness that they may enact violence upon your person."

In hearing that from Offutt, although it brought chuckles from the others, Abraham did not laugh at all. What a marvel, to speak so fine. Abraham recalled how well Allen had spoken. And he recalled how he, Abraham, had copied Allen's words and way of talking. Now it was Offutt whom Abraham was going to study. Abraham considered his good luck. It had been a hard winter. Now, instead of packing up as planned and returning to Indiana to farm, he was traveling down that once-accursed long river, learning advanced rhetoric once again. The Mississippi was his classroom. He needed no other. No matter in which place a student read, the book and the student were the same. No matter where the teacher stood, even on the banks of a river amidst felled trees, the student could learn. It was all up to the student. Abraham never wanted to stop his learning.

On Congress land, in their lean-to, Abraham held forth to John Roll, that he ought to keep up on books and try and learn to cipher and to write.

"Anyone who wants to be more than a plowman has to become familiar with the written word. It is a great invention, probably the greatest of all of man's inventions," Abraham told Roll, whose smile did not cease.

"Am I ridiculous in your eyes?" Abraham asked.

"No."

"You smile."

"I smile because I never know what you are going to come out with. You talk well."

You talk well. Abraham savored the sound of that. In his life, compliments had been rare and usually related to his agricultural productivity.

"Why is writing so amazing?" Roll asked.

Abraham said, "Why, through writing we are able to talk with the dead, the absent, the unborn, are we not, John?"

"I suppose."

"And with writing, one inventor may thus communicate to another inventor, who may build upon his inventions and make this world a happier place for all."

Roll pondered a minute and then, smiling broadly, said, "A regular Utopia. How close you expect we will come to Heaven?"

"I venture a good deal closer with writing than without it, John Roll."

Another thought struck Roll.

"You done much writing, yourself, Abe?"

"I have. I have. I have even been published."

That was news.

"Do tell," Roll urged Abraham.

"Lots of letters for friends and neighbors. Receipts for my family," Abraham said, choosing not to say the receipts were all for his illiterate father. "Couple of my letters were published in newspapers. And one of my writings is in the public records of the Decatur court-house, an appraisal of an estray mare. I both wrote and signed it."

Roll immediately thought of the most current controversy in the county, the vacancy in the constabulary. He wondered if Abraham was not the answer to prayers.

"Maybe you can help us out of our fix before you leave down river," Roll said.

Abraham asked, "What fix?"

"Our constable quit and left town, went west like everybody these days. We need a new one, of course, and plenty of us could use a job like that."

"What's it pay?"

"I'm not talking about you being constable, Abe. I'm saying you could write the petition," John said.

"Oh," Abraham said, brightening when he realized that he would be downriver. "I couldn't do the job anyway. I'll be away."

"Sure, you will. We need the county commissioners to act and name another constable," John said.

"Why didn't somebody else write it already?" Abraham said, feeling suspicious despite John Rolls appearing to be honest enough.

"It's a sore point around here, everybody is looking at each other because anybody who writes the petition would look like they were aiming for the job, you know. But everybody would sign, you know. If a stranger wrote it up."

Abraham said, "A qualified stranger, Rolls, not being a thief, a rowdy or a drunk."

Rolls slapped Abraham on the back and said that he was just the one. So it was that rainy morning, at John Roll's request, Abraham wrote up a short petition. It was addressed to the Honorable County Commissioners of Sangamon County. Further, dated at its top March 11, 1831, Abraham wrote out "Whereas it is represented to us that there is a vacancy in the office of constable," and the commissioners are authorized by "Statute in such cases made and provided," that the County Commissioners ought to fill "said vacancy with some suitable person."

Hanks and Johnny were already working on the flatboat when Abraham hollered over, "You all right with me signing your names? onto a petition to appoint a new constable?"

Johnston said, "Go ahead, just spell it right. And my middle initial is D. You remember? John D. Johnston. J-o-h-n-s-t-o-n."

"Hanks?" Abraham asked.

"I don't want our card games interrupted or interfered with," Hanks said.

"Don't worry about that," Roll said. "We'll get a card-loving constable. Nobody but loves cards around here. Even the Baptists."

Abraham signed his own name, A. Lincoln, as well as John Hanks and John D. Johnston, then gave it to Roll to gather more signatures before rising, putting away his pen and ink, and taking off his shirt to make dust in the world. The morning was fresh and new.

CHAPTER FOURTEEN

At the sawmill, Abraham, while waiting for their timber to turn into beams, boards, planks and slats, had the inclination and the time to sit and talk with Sawtelle, the operator of Kirkpatrick's mill but he was polite. He waited for Sawtelle to speak first.

"I heard of you, Lincoln," Sawtelle said. "I heard that you can write and that you made up a petition to name a new constable."

"That was me. You in the running?" Abraham asked.

"I am. Why did you write that petition?"

"To put the commissioners to the task."

"But why?"

"They are elected to perform it."

Sawtelle was dissatisfied with anyone doing good for good's sake. He remained suspicious of Abraham Lincoln. What was in it for him?

Sawtelle asked, "How about a petition for sawmills? Fools oppose mills."

"Where?"

"They don't want a grist mill down river, at New Salem village. People are squawking about a dam there, as if it was dangerous to boats."

"Oh, a land-owner can build a dam, can't he?" Abraham asked, as if it was no controversy at all.

"Land owner already has. But they talk about taking Rutledge's dam down."

"Talk is not action," Abraham said.

Sawtelle was finding it hard to win an argument with this boy.

"Talk leads to opinion that leads to laws that lead to action. You prohibit a dam, you know, we'd have problems. How do you have a mill without a dam? And without a grist mill, New Salem has no flour and the farmers can't put up barrels of corn meal to sell at market. We got to live on the river together or it will be what it was, a river running through woods."

Abraham was, all that while, listening and learning. He conceived the proposition that a river was charged with public use. He deducted further from this premise that no one party ought to have complete control. After a little more thought, he also concluded that no productive purpose ought to be thwarted. If he did not draw up a petition here and now he would do so some later day. If anyone wished to dam a stream to start a mill, or something along that line, Abraham would be a supporter. What about a bridge over the Mississippi? Wouldn't that be something?

That afternoon, of all people, Johnny suggested a means by which they might raise a sum of money themselves. Actually, nobody would claim credit later. The initial idea had been at first kind of vague.

CHAPTER FIFTEEN

"What do we do to pass time between sundown and sleep?" Abraham asked.

"Well, I don't want to hear your Jew's harp," Hanks told Abraham, shaking his head.

"And I don't want to hear you recite," Johnny said, "or your stories."

"What do you suggest then, Johnny, cards?" Abraham asked, his hand furtively pressed on Hanks's side. Hanks said nothing but, clued in, observed Johnny.

Johnny said, "Cards, sure. Hey, whyn't we have a regular game and get men out here to place a wager or two?"

Hanks played along, scratching his nose and looking blank, asking, "But we could lose money."

"The house never loses," Johnny said. "The house always wins. Pa said. That's what people won't believe but it's true."

"Pa told you not to gamble."

Johnny was not stumped. He said back, "Gambling is risky but owning the gambling-house is a sure thing."

"It's too far out here," Abraham said.

"That's why they'd come, Abe, to get away from their farms for an hour or two. They don't all want to stay by the fire reading books like you. What do you say, Cousin Hanks?" Johnny asked.

Hanks said, "I think it'd be too much work. I can't shuffle. You?"

"Can I shuffle?" Johnny asked. "Listen, you just watch me."

He looked through his sack until he found a deck of cards. He placed them on a flat board and shuffled several rounds, then dealt out hands like lightning.

"I never saw anything like that," Hanks said.

"Me neither," Abraham said, stifling a guffaw.

"Then you ain't been watching when I play Pa."

"You win against your Pa?" Hanks asked.

"Sometimes," Johnny said.

"Well, if you think it would be a good idea, you be the dealer and I'll make the coffee and chops or something," Abraham said.

"I don't want grease on the cards," Johnny said.

Hanks said, "Something simpler, biscuits maybe, and mind the salt. I'll teach the games. We may want Roll and his friend, Caleb Carmen, watch the money and the door, you know, against any cheats, signals or cards up the sleeve."

Ever after, Johnny claimed it was his idea and neither Hanks nor Abraham disputed it. Starting with his deck of cards – eventually they bought five more — nightly games of eight and milldam were held at their shanty. Hanks placidly and patiently taught rules of the games to the farmers whom Roll and Carmen got to escort out of the shanty on rowdy nights. They would eat free treats, sugar-biscuits and bacon fried up hot by Abraham, and they'd swill down a half-tumbler of diluted whiskey "for gratis," all the while playing cards in the dim light of two candles as long as their eyelids stayed up.

Johnny was right. Luck really did favor the house. After a week of Johnny dealing, they were ahead by almost twelve dollars, a fleece-lined jacket with a tear, a nice and almost new small pair of child's boots (which they would only receive after their bearer swore that his child had outgrown them), several jack-knives and a spoon that was either silver or pewter, nobody being certain which. When Roll filled a chair one time, they won Roll's gold watch but gave it back. Of all prizes won at the card table, Abraham claimed only an old black hat with a broad brim that fit him.

You only have to get rich once, Gentry had told Abraham in Indiana. Gentry's old man quoted the Bible, "Cast your bread upon the waters. Some will return manifold, some not at all." Hanks and Johnny were paying Abraham two bits a week for the cooking and their laundering. With that and his share of the gambling revenues, Abraham could buy goods to trade on his own account downriver.

His mind raced ahead of everything to the end of their trip, coming back on the steamboat. Abraham would arrange with the captain to work for his passage. He could redeem his ticket with the purser. His wages as cook, gambling dollars, the contract wages and bonus, his own side trades, the ticket redeemed, he would have a stake. In St. Louis, Abraham could disembark to chop wood or be hired by a blacksmith or a horse-breeder. By the Fourth of July, Abraham might knock on his family's cabin door a rich man bearing gifts for all, with money ahead for Indiana. That would be sweet.

CHAPTER SIXTEEN

Meanwhile, John Roll, completed what he had begun as a lark, taking down a good tree and turning it into a canoe with seats carved out. Walter Carman, younger brother of Caleb, a settler back in New Salem, and Johnny Johnston, whom he'd quickly befriended, hounded Roll every day for the honor of being the first ride out. He gave them both his promise of first ride in his new canoe. The day Roll finished, the river had risen. Possibly cresting, the whole bottom was now flooded, even the tallest bank trees standing like islands. The current was likewise swift and strong. Roll suggested to the boys that they wait. It was advice never welcome to the young.

"Let's see what she is made of, good day for it," Walter insisted. "Johnny can row and I'll pilot. Look at Johnny. Ain't he strong?"

Roll shook his head at the roiling waters in flood. Lincoln and Hanks, closed-mouthed sages, hung back from glory-seeking.

"Not as strong as some," Roll said, looking over at Abraham, standing on the bank with Hanks, silent before the rushing river. Catching Roll's drift, Johnny resented that look.

"You just watch us, Roll," Johnny said.

The three older men, Roll, Hanks and Abraham, witnessed as Walter and Johnny pushed the canoe, which was by no means light. They got it down through the rooted soil between trees into the water and then jumped aboard with a hooray. Had the water been dead calm — which it was not — the pair of them would have been likely to have enjoyed themselves. Instead, clawed out spinning quickly by devious and contradictory surface and subsurface currents in conflict, waves lapping up over the sides, they bailed and yelled curses at indistinct enemies.

After nearly overturning twice, they finally did overturn. The canoe sank beneath them as they foundered in the icy waters of the flooded river. When he surfaced, Walter was screaming, Johnny bobbed, his head visible but not his hands, looking pained but mute a moment before he stretched out and paddled his arms against raging water.

Ashore, Abraham shouted for them to swim and head for the tree. He pointed slightly downstream. Not far was an elm about half-way submerged. What could be seen was full of likely branches and holds. Abraham saw their only hope instantly. Roll's canoe was gone.

Following Abraham's plan, the two young men more floated than swam, but hit, held and scrambled up the elm tree and out of the waters. Breathless and coughing in its branches, they were safe for the moment. The tree was straight and steady. However, the river raged and there remained an incalculable danger. Their refuge could be torn up by its roots. Then, borne swiftly downstream, they would be taken away with the tree, mere flies caught in its web. They had seen such sights while chopping and planing on shore. Many big trees seemingly less vulnerable had already gone down the Sangamon just that way.

Abraham, by whose instruction the boys had been treed, faced the issue of how to get the boys down in current almost a hundred feet from shore before the sun went down.

In that, he was assisted. Hanks volunteered to go out on a log. With Roll helping the strongest man, Abraham rigged a log with several spliced long ropes. Tossing the ropes over his shoulders, he pulled and hauled that log, cutting a groove in the soil on the way to the current edge of the river. Once Hanks, with one oar, was seated — he decided it would be safer not to be fastened or roped to the log — Hanks and the log were launched, shoved out from far upstream of the elm tree. Abraham then paid out rope while Hanks kicked, splashed, rowed and squirmed, trying to maintain a seat on a log swirling and turning like a bucking bronco in boiling waters. It turned over not long after launch, dipping Hanks, who lost the oar. He clung manfully to the log as it was hauled back with the straining duo of Abraham and Roll.

"I will venture it next," Abraham said, patting Hanks on the shoulder. "You help with the rope, I'll need you."

With Abraham now as the log's new pilot and captain, straddling it better with his long legs and balancing it, making adjustments like an acrobat as it tipped or began to move in any direction, the log went out over rapids as if on smooth waters. Strung out nearly to the end of the triple-spliced ropes before he reached the men in the tree, Abraham directed first Walter, then Johnny to climb down and grip the log while he tied thin ropes about their hands to the rigging around the log. For them, it would be safer to be tied. After that, it would be a matter of swift hauling back on the rope.

The log and the three men came back to shore.

Holding Abraham's shoulders in his shaking hands, Walter bowed his head, all but kissing Abraham. Walter said, "I owe you my life, Abe. I'm going to tell my brother up in New Salem. He's a constable up there and a millwright. That place is going to grow. You go up and see Caleb Carman, he'll do right by you."

"You owe me nothing."

Johnny said nothing.

"Who's going to pay for my canoe?" Roll asked.

Nobody laughed. Roll was serious.

"I'll cut cards for it with you," Abraham said.

Roll backed off.

"I'd as soon lose my canoe than risk another card game."

Everybody laughed.

Abraham had left his broad-brimmed, low-crowned old black hat ashore during his adventure. He now grabbed it up and hastily crowned Roll with it before Roll could object. As he began to squawk, Abraham said, "It's yours now. You can't wear a canoe. Bargain in your favor, Roll."

Roll frowned, took the hat off and threw it back to Abraham, who caught it.

"It don't fit," Roll said. "I can't wear a hat that don't fit either. Somebody owes me a canoe."

"River goes down, we'll look for it," Abraham said in a pleasant, cheerful tone, adjusting the hat to set level on his brow. Under it, he resembled a Quaker going to meeting.

He smiled. Two men were alive who might have drowned, one of them his step brother. Abraham had spared his parents grief. And he had a new friend in the growing village of New Salem, whether Caleb Carman knew it or not.

Maybe he could get a job at the mill with Caleb. Abraham wanted to learn about machines. He could invent all the plank sails he wanted, if he was going to get ahead, he knew that it would have to be by serving more people than four men on a flatboat.

CHAPTER SEVENTEEN

One day at noon break, Roll asked anybody listening and nobody in particular, "You going to the show?"

"What show?" Johnny asked, at the end of a plank. For a week now, he and Abraham had been carrying planks from a pile that was fast turning into a flat-boat. In one instance, Abraham had an idea and implemented it before checking with Roll. Roll agreed it was a great convenience. Abraham had measured and sized a plank. He then sawed it and punched a hole through, which he filed to be smooth on all edges. With two big brass hinges and screws, he fixed it in place on the inner stern. If it were flipped up, it hung over the end of the craft without slipping. With it, they were a floating privy.

"No flies on you, Abe," Roll said after a demonstration.

On most boats the act of defecation involved hanging precariously over the edge of the boat and hoping not to fall in or leave a mark. Success was uneven. Abraham's invention of a hinged hole-board was a novelty to Roll.

"You might patent it," Roll said.

"It shall be my gift to the world," Abraham said, laughing. But he was proud of his invention, demonstrating upon no excuse to Offutt, to Walter Carman, and to any visitor.

Done with the hinged hole-board, they were not done with the boat. After a long week of labor and some inventing, though, they were more than ready for some recreation besides card games.

Roll, who could read, knew from a posting down at the grocery that Saturday afternoon for women and children, Saturday evening for men there was to be a show.

""A magician, Orlando of Cairo. He juggles, too, I think," Roll said. "Women pay twenty cents, children go free. Gents at night are twenty-five cents. I imagine there will be jokes at the evening show that the wives and kids will not hear."

"How long'll it last?" Johnny asked, thinking about the steep price of the show.

Roll said, "Got to be a good, long show for a quarter-dollar. We'd run him out of town on a rail if it doesn't go an hour."

"You going?" Johnny asked.

"I am," Roll said. "To see a good show or a good mob. We take it personal when anybody suckers us in Sangamo County, you betcha."

He rubbed a fist he made as if to savor an old grudge or an old memory.

"I'm going," Abraham said.

Johnny said, "I am, too. I never saw a magician. Wonder if he'll do card tricks."

Rolls dismissed card tricks as the least interesting kind of tricks, being tricks even they could perform for one another "any rainy day."

Rolls said he rated a good juggler above every other skill, or an acrobat. He saw one who was both, flinging knives in the air, doing hand-stands and somersaults and catching the falling knives.

"Nothing better," Roll said. "Nobody moved an inch or took a willful breath, only gasped when the fellow caught a knife we were certain he had forgot or was sure to miss even if he tried. Quite a show. That was only a dime, though, because it was short. I went back for another dime and was well pleased to pay it. My wife used to tease me about my 'twenty cent juggler,' she called him. Nesbitt was his name. The Amazing Nesbitt, he was, too. When we get short of cash, she still says, 'Oh, that's on account of your Nesbitt.' But I never regretted it, never."

That evening after sunset, two flaming torches were stuck in the ground as a sort of official entrance to the grocery. Roll was one of the first in line. Abraham, Hanks and Johnny with him, got into line. A drummer was beating an increasingly faster-paced cadence somewhere inside the grocery where, on its second floor, the merchant had cleared away furniture and set up chairs, benches and boxes in a circle around a three-box stage where the magician would perform.

"Offutt's missing a good show," Johnny said.

"I imagine he is seeing what he wants to see," Abraham said, winking at Hanks, who smiled. They had Offutt pinned as a ladies' man. Offutt's frequent and lengthy business trips afforded him many opportunities to see and even to partake in amateur performances.

Upstairs, the show this evening began with the magician's appearance, suddenly from behind a fold of curtain unnoticed at the side.

"Good evening, gentlemen," the magician said in a loud and clear manner. His long-fingered hands were folded into one another.

"Good evening, gentlemen," the magician repeated, and only then did they all understand that it was a greeting to which they were intended to respond, and they good eveninged back.

He then walked forward, chin up, head straight. Atop his head, itself segmented by a broad, black thin-tipped moustache perched atop his upper lip, was a sort of swaddling cloth wrapped into a bandanna-tuck, in front of which some sort of gemstone or jewelry caught the flickers of the many candles and gleamed back.

"I am Orlando of Cairo. I am learned in the arts of the Middle East and Holy Land. I welcome you to sights never before seen by the mortal men of the Sangamo Valley, things that my psychic energy affords me to perform no more than twice in a day. I confess to you that I practice, in two words, the black arts."

"That's three words," Johnny whispered. "And it's Sangamo County, not Sangamo Valley."

"Hush," Hanks said.

"'The-black-arts' is three words," Johnny said.

"Pay attention," Abraham said.

"I am," Johnston said, "more attention than anybody else, it seems like."

As they whispered, the magician stepped up. After mounting the stage, after a pop and a burst of smoke, suddenly from out of nowhere, he was holding in his hands a bouquet of flowers that, upon his tossing the bouquet into the air, somehow vanished.

"Ohh," the men said, unable to imagine how it was done.

"I bet it was a hidden string," Johnny said.

"One more word and I'll make *you* disappear," Hanks said, sounding serious.

That was the end of interruptions by Johnny.

After a juggling act which began with one item tossed by a member of the audience, and then another, until the magician was juggling five differently-shaped and sized items, a jack-knife, a watch with a chain, spectacles, a pen and a cigar, all for a good minute or two, the men applauded and cheered mightily and stamped their feet.

Roll's loud voice was audible above the rest, hollering, "You are good."

Bringing out Indian clubs of his own after returning the borrowed items, the magician juggled into a blurring frenzy, the clubs whirling about him indistinguishably until he slowed, stopped and held them, two in one hand and three in the other. The reaction was even more overwhelming.

Roll again hooted and kept repeating, "I told you. I told you."

Next, the magician opened a box to show that it was empty, closed it up and said several exotic words. Abraham could hear Johnny repeating in a low whisper, trying to memorize the secret charm. With a few waves and casts of his hands over the box, the magician opened it and two white doves flew up and landed, one on each shoulder.

This trick netted Orlando more approving gestures.

"Has anyone here a hat that I may borrow?" Orlando asked.

"What you going to do with it?" Roll asked, his straw hat plainly upon his head.

"A fair question, friend," the magician said. "I am going to cook two eggs in it, over this candle here."

Suddenly, a candle appeared in one hand while, snapping his fingers over an apparently concealed loco, he had a flame to light it.

"Here's a hat, mister," Johnny said, waving a hat, having taken Abraham's broad-brimmed, low-crowned old black hat up and off Abraham's head.

"Hold on," Abraham said.

The magician said, "Oh, now, I need help from somebody, sir. May I not have the temporary loan of your hat?"

"It ain't the hat I'm concerned about, it's your eggs," Abraham said, getting up a good laugh in the crowd. Abraham then shrugged and waved his hand that Johnny could give his hat on up to the magician on stage, who did, indeed, in a few moments, perform a trick by cracking two eggs, apparently dropping them into the hat, which led to the crowd noise of *aww*. This was followed by the usual hocus-pocus, strange hand gestures and a little swirling of Abraham's hat over the candle, from which the magician seemed to extract a couple of eggs fried together.

"Would you like the eggs, sir?" Orlando asked Abraham.

"I just want the hat, Mr. Orlando," Abraham said, to cheers and laughter.

The magician said, "I am here to grant wishes."

He then stepped off the stage and, with an ostentatious low bow, stretched his arm and held out Abraham's hat for him to take. As he offered the hat, he may have whispered, or merely lean toward Abraham's ear, but it was difficult to tell anything even as close as a foot or two from Abraham and the magician.

Abraham took back the hat.

"Check it out," someone yelled.

"Best inspect," Hanks said.

Abraham looked the hat over carefully, feeling it inside and out, holding it up as the magician rose to standing position.

"Well, sir?" Orlando asked Abraham.

"It seems no worse than it was," Abraham said.

That was the crowd's last laugh. He now performed before the stage, cheek-to-jowl with the front row. He would occasionally begin with a display of his hands, indicating that her had nothing in them or up his sleeves. His remaining several tricks caused gasps and "how did he do that" as one rapidly followed another. With the magician's final trick, he stepped up on the stage only to doff his own tall hat and to bow as they applauded.

"Thank you, thank you all. Anyone traveling may see me at the Hotel Tremont in St. Louis or, if you are going by steamship, you might see my act on the *Tecumseh* to New Orleans. Good evening, all."

After the show, they spent no more time in the grocery, although Roll and others went for the whiskey barrel and ladled freely at a nickel a ladle.

"He was good," Hanks said.

Johnny asked, "Wasn't he, though? And how'd he do that with your hat, Abe? I can't figure out none of them tricks."

Abraham said, "Well, maybe he is a real magician and practices genuine magic."

"Do you think?" Johnny asked.

Hanks stifled guffaws, but Abraham looked straight forward and severe. The magician, in giving him his hat, had whispered, "I see bloodshed. I am sorry."

He could not see the future, Abraham thought. And yet what he said Abraham had heard in a Voice in Indiana. What the magician seemed to have seen could not be and yet, Abraham wondered, why did the magician see fit to select him, to warn him, of everyone there? On the contrary, too, how many of the other things he saw or knew were no more real than the magician's act? The stars twinkled on the three as they followed paths to their shanty. In that darkness, Abraham was lost in thought. Questions ran through his head: who would bleed? would someone die? would he have to kill someone? Indians? It was only a step farther to recall the rain barrel. Some visions came true.

He stepped inside the shanty, one foot after another. He was glad to take off his boots and let his stockings dry.

"My turn at the fire," Abraham said, although it was Johnny's. Abraham expected not to sleep. He might as well tend the fire.

Johnny made no objection.

CHAPTER EIGHTEEN

The day dawned hot and sticky when the boat was ready enough to be fitted out for business with cargo.

Three families came to deliver goods contracted for by Offutt.

All of them, without exception, stayed a few more hours to watch the excitement of loading up a flatboat to go downriver. All through that day, the busy crew now including farm-boys hired for the day.

They loaded five tiers of shelves in the large cargo hold. The lowest, coolest tier was for barrels of apples, next up potatoes in burlap sacks, on top of them sacks of flour, then the most-easily-reachable fourth tier, shoulder-high, for anything cloth, quilts, blankets, pillow-cases, of which Offutt had a slew to trade at farms all along the river. They also were to trade cordage, buckets and brooms, which they packed closely, and stray miscellaneous shoes, boots, baby clothes, laces, percussion caps, two crates of patent medicines, a whole dental kit with pliers, a flute, a violin with a bow but no strings, candles, mirrors – the little mirrors were printed with Offutt's name and lettering about his enterprises — and animal traps. Offutt regaled anybody who would listen about his hopes, how he'd like to trade and get peaches, pilot bread, whiskey or brandy, lard and hides or fur from the farms along the river. Up over atop of everything, not quite filling the fifth tier – room for more goods later — were barrels of pork on one side and sacks of coarse-ground corn on the other, provender for the live hogs. In the front hold, their kegs of water, their heaviest cargo, they stacked equally on both sides, roping an aisle for passage. Next, just behind the ladder and the hatch they'd open for ventilation, they moved aboard twenty small pigs, with more to come. They scrambled and played in their large stall freely for now. Quarters would be tight later.

In the rear hold, where the crew would sleep and cook, they stowed their supplies including tinware with which to cook and to eat, beans, slabs of bacon, a small ham, six small pots, three containing honey, three containing blackberry jam, three fortuitous barrels of sauerkraut that Offutt bought cheap from a passing German teamster, dozens of onions, two sacks of carrots, a barrel of buckwheat flour they had to stand outside the curtained pantry, filled with oatmeal, eggs, cheese, sugar, cinnamon, pepper and salt, tea, coffee, saleratus for corn bread and a few others spices. They had a cubby-hole for soap, candles, locos, a comb, brush, whistle and a jew's harp, the latter being Abraham's one musical accomplishment. Nothing made Hanks, Abraham or Johnny any happier than the sight of their pantry, after such a winter.

It was finally, late in the day, nearing sunset, and Offutt decided that they had time to launch. With an audience still standing, John Roll nodded that the rest were in place with their ropes and poles and Offutt took a swing with his mallet. He squarely knocked off a holding pin and the loaded flatboat began sliding down toward the river. It made such a splash that some gasped and others screamed, but all was well. The flatboat did not tip or sink. The crowd converged upon Offutt, shaking his hand, swatting his back, yelling "good luck, good luck." He received all of this with hearty, nodding pleasure before wading out and holding out his arms to be heaved up aboard by Hanks on one side and Abraham on the other. It was as if a soul were being raised to Heaven.

As they left Sangamon Town, Captain Offutt commenced to sing:

Despise me not, my carnal friends,
Lest you despise my Lord:
He bids me in the water go,
And I'll obey his word.

The crowd cheered, loathe still to disperse until he was out of sight and hearing.

The flatboat was a much larger craft than Abraham had ever been on. Now something he had built of such a large size was properly afloat. He knew its whole genesis, from tree to plank, to construction to being filled with cargo and crewed by the four of them. It seemed a miracle to be floating, drifting now, without incident or a single care, the captain singing. Unlike the boat he'd shared with Allen Gentry, which had but one warped-wood floor, a railing and a sort of pilot-house or shanty structure in back for weather and to sleep, this one was ark-like.

Abraham looked behind him as he stood poling at the bow. It had two or three layers of deck depending on how you counted, a foredeck at the bow with torch-sockets – Abraham had to ask what they were as they were drilled – the lower middle deck for cargo, including live, squealing cargo, a sturdy warehouse-on-water with railings and shelves, and the rear cabin or bunkhouse, which Roll had seen to waterproofing himself with thick coats of creosote.

Abraham knew that only two wooden slats for bunks had been built on the belief that no more than two at a time would be off duty. For space-saving, innovative Roll designed a series of pegs from which sacks or other items might be hung, a set-off platform for a couple of buckets, and a cabinet with two shelves for food storage.

Later, Abraham would note that Offutt could, and did, slide his tin box of money underneath the lower bunk. By Offutt's orders, the top deck was designed to bear Abraham's improvised plank sails and also a flagpole.

"We're going down river under 'Old Glory', boys," Offutt had declared, his finger pointed upward, his expression beatific and patriotic. If it would be so, they had yet to purchase a flag.

CHAPTER NINETEEN

At first, the cabin of the flatboat had smelled of a mix of fresh-cut wood and creosote but, when Johnston dropped and smashed a jar of Pennsylvania Dutch pickles, the smell of vinegar was dominant. They also thereafter had to watch where they stepped in bare feet or stockings. Johnston's vision in the dimly-lit cabin (which had a sliding-door opening for air and sunlight) had not enabled him to find every piece or sliver of glass in the cracks and crevices of the back. Nobody, the whole voyage, ever felt entirely comfortable walking over its surface.

The smell changed for the worse. The fresh wood and creosote, and even the vinegar, faded before the incoming tide of male intimacy. Mississippi water was so muddy that one could not clean oneself or shave without a gritty coating lingering on one's skin.

It was common, of course, that river boatmen were distinguishable by their beards and untamed hair. They were loud, yelling being the favored form of communication on the raucous river, in fair weather or foul. Boatmen were hardly dirtier or much smellier than many a farmer. What the boatmen, on their first voyage or their fiftieth, truly had in common were the dangers of the river. They all understood hostility and a sense of the land world's resentment and active enmity. They might become prey for thieves or murderers at any time. They were targets thought to be vulnerable because: who would miss them? how would their murders ever become known?

The dangers outweighed the discomforts (largely ignored) of living on cramped, usually damp, frequently filthy, and uncomfortable flatboats. Sleeping was rationed, eating was hurried and exotic.

All soon fell in with custom in evacuation of the bowels and urination. All functions were done in open air, night or day. One simply ignored the fact that one's neighbor, with whom one was conversing, was at the side of the flatboat occasionally grunting as he managed to evade constipation for that day. Constipation traveled with them all, given the hard tack and salt beef or other provisions that combined as their stomach-blocking fare. Everybody had a different folk remedy for it and none of the remedies worked very regularly.

Curses were another matter. Sailors at sea and bargemen on the Thames aside, no men on earth equaled the gusto with which the boatmen cursed. Any landsman who listened for five minutes to boatmen talking would be dazzled by the extent to which the world was so densely covered with scatological, profane and derisive words, terms unknown on land but circulating on the river like water itself. Abraham was alone on the *Ark,* even ahead of Hanks, in not falling into the habit of cursing. Offutt, Hanks and Johnny were akin to ministers, forever speaking of God, Heaven and Jesus in a constant flow. Abraham so famously did not join them that Hanks asked once why he did not swear.

"Nobody but us to hear you," Hanks said, with Abraham then setting their largest, tallest plank sail up on the topdeck.

"I don't want the habit," Abraham said. "My mind being like a steel plate, once you scratch something on it, it is there forever. I don't want the habit. I should find myself swearing to Ma to pass the bread."

In this instance, he did add a curse word, which made his remark so funny.

"I understand," Hanks said, and so did he.

CHAPTER TWENTY

Having launched the *Ark* so grandly on April 17th, Abraham recalled the sad, little splash he and Allen Gentry had made in 1828. Almost unwitnessed, only James Gentry watched solemnly, surveying his investment. Even Abraham's father had gone back to the farm.

That had been Pigeon Creek, Johnny riding off on the back of a horse with Pa, neither one having interest in watching the launch. Abraham thought that Pa was then probably making the wagons in which to flee Indiana. However, touch would only go so far in carpentry. Measured by feel and not by sight, the big wheels Pa made lacked circularity. Iron rims would not cure this, they'd wobbled *dukkha –dukkha –dukkha* from Indiana to Illinois.

Aboard the *Ark*, Abraham was greatly enjoying Offutt's company. Offutt was the sort to be as tickled as a child, or as his sister, Sarah, when they were both young and he'd pretended to read the Bible and made up stories from memory and imagination. Nobody else, Hanks included, had ever approved of Abraham's way of Bible reading and mocking. Offutt was different, just right in his taste that way. The night before launch, Abraham had read aloud the story of Adam and the crusty, spouty, blasting God of the Garden of Eden. Hanks said later that Offutt was leading him down "the primrose path" and Abraham thought Hanks was probably right. Maybe Offutt was not an ideal or perfectly admirable fellow. Abraham replied to Hanks, "He's a likeable fellow."

Like Hanks, Abraham knew that Offutt drank too much, was casual about promises, and even rejoiced at cheating people in deals. All that said, Abraham had never met anybody like Offutt. Glad of the trip, grateful for the opportunity, Abraham studied him closely.

They soon, within five miles, approached a warehouse beside the river.

"We may stop and do some business here," Offutt said, guiding them toward the pier outside the place. Under a huge sign **"HACKETT'S,"** the place offered grain storage, milling and had some corn, although at the price of twenty-five cents per bushel as posted. He handed the tiller over to Abraham.

"Holloa, you Hackett?" Offutt said, his hands up making a speaking funnel around his mouth.

"I am Hackett," a man said.

Hackett did not rise from his chair, tiled back to the front wall of his warehouse. He was wearing a straw hat and chewing.

"What for corn?" Offutt yelled.

"Twenty-five," the man said, pointing toward the posted rate.

"Can't stop for twenty-five," Offutt shouted, taking the tiller back and steering out toward mid-stream.

The man stood and took two steps forward from his chair.

"Twenty cents," he yelled.

Offutt had just time, with a veering movement, to edge up to the end of the pier with his flatboat. Abraham and Johnny tied the craft to upright studs, snugly fixing it.

"Now, Offutt, do your best," Offutt said to himself, Abraham listening.

They had to have corn for the New Orleans trade. Corn was a huge part of the plan. Offutt told Abraham that he aimed to get as high as fifty cents a bushel, if so, making the whole trip profitable by corn alone. Offutt figured on a thousand bushels, paying no more than twelve-and-a-half cents a bushel. No telling how the corn harvest was downriver, or prices. "I may find the price in New Orleans is twenty cents," Offutt said. "I've got to cut close as I can up here."

Climbing up and over to the pier, Offutt walked right up to Hackett. He then said, "Don't riose, don't rise," as he entrapped Hackett's right hand, pulled it up and heartily shook with both hands. Abraham next heard Offutt say, "Denton Offutt, sir, of Kentucky, pleased to make your acquaintance. I think that we are both fair men of business. No doubt, you have been asking twenty cents all winter from folks who only paid in six-per-cent promissory notes and may not pay at all. You and I both know that five folks are leaving Illinois for every two coming in from Kentucky. Your corn dry?"

"You can check. I assure you this place is dry. I have not had the fires out the whole winter."

"My notes are good. My name is my bond."

"Mister Offutt, let us not dally and dicker over notes and interest. I will give you my best price ever of fifteen cents a bushel, cash on the barrelhead."

"Well, cash. I see. I hadn't been thinking of cash. Cash."

He looked for paper and pencil in his coat pockets.

"Cash, Mr. Hackett? Suppose you meet my price. Let me do a little calculating."

Offutt scratched out some cryptic figures on a scrap.

He put his hand under his chin.

He shook his head.

He did more figuring.

He scratched his head.

He sighed.

"Way I figure it, the winter's over," Offutt said, looking up at Hackett. It was a message between two knowing businessmen. In other words, the winter being over with, plenty of corn from this wet spring would steeply cut down the price of the dry corn Hackett was hoarding. "The winter's over" implied that the tide was about to turn in buyers' favor.

Hackett dropped his crossed arms down from his chest.

"You figured that out, did you? On paper?"

Offutt had amused him. Offutt knew when to strike.

Offutt said, "I'll give you payment in specie, here and today, ten cents a bushel, but I got to get 800 bushels. That's eighty dollars, American, in hand now."

"I only sell by the thousand at ten cents. A hundred dollars, cash in hand."

Offutt sighed, mumbling to himself and scratching his head until finally he stuck out his hand to shake, saying, "A thousand bushels of dry corn at ten cents a bushel, cash in hand, today, now. A hundred dollars if you help with the loading."

Holding his hand out but not yet shaking, Hackett said, "Help, but I will not do more than my share. You've got a crew."

"All right. A thousand bushels of dry corn, ten cents a bushel, cash, today, and you help with the loading but only your share, no more, no less. Using your wheelbarrow. And throw in a bottle of corn whiskey. You're a poor businessman if you do not have some. My final offer or I am off to another vendor, Mr. Hackett."

"Deal," Hackett said, laughing, shaking his head. He pointed and said, "You are a sharp one, Offutt."

"I shall check my funds on hand, which I keep with me aboard this boat I own, specially built for me, brand new."

"Check funds? You said cash."

"So much cash as I possess shall be yours. I may need some small degree of your trust on a promissory note."

Hackett was caught between red-faced anger and laughing out loud now. Abraham watched, wondering what would happen next.

"Twenty dollar promissory note at six per cent," Hackett grumbled.

"Thirty dollars. Think of the added interest. Atop seventy dollars cash this day," Offutt said. "Let us shake on it."

Hackett and he, after all, had yet to shake. Hackett grabbed Offutt's hand now quickly, lest some new factor be suggested in their shifting deal. Now they had a deal.

Hanks, Abraham, Johnny and Hackett worked to load three-bushel and five-bushel sacks of corn into the hold, separated and dry. They heard Offutt singing his hymns. A hundred dollars changed hands, smiles all around, and time passed quickly over glasses raised, although Abraham declined anything but water. Then they untied, cast off and were on the river again.

"Good bargaining," Abraham told Offutt.

Offutt winked and said, "Nothing you can't learn, my boy. Keep your eyes and ears open, this is your education."

CHAPTER TWENTY-ONE

Abraham felt as if he had entered the ark in the flood. He rose up and away. The river carried him away from all earthly things and concerns and lesser pleasures. Afloat, Abraham, for the joy of it, stood atop the boat. Twenty feet above the surface, the tall man commanded a view of rushing water ahead and around and behind. On the Gentry boat, Abraham had felt himself one with the river surface, a water skate, when not dipping partly below as a species of driftwood. On Offutt's *Ark of the New Covenant*, Abraham enjoyed a breeze-borne sensation transcendent and wonderful, above any earthly life, in a surviving pocket of Heaven. He adjusted the sails, fitting a thin triangle of wood into one of three front slots.

On this journey, Abraham was an inventor performing experiments. He did not know if plank sails would work. He knew that canvas was rare and that the nearest sail loft seemed to be in Philadelphia. Plank sails on thousands of flatboats headed for New Orleans might make him a rich and famous inventor. Or the plank sail he made and adjusted could be the last plank sail in America.

The boat, too was, an invention in part. John Roll had designed little conveniences for them, modifying the generality of mere "flatboat" into the *Ark* to suit them on this trip in particular, with their hog pen, their sleeping shifts, the flagpole Offutt wanted. It worked. It floated. It drifted. It did not lean or wobble. No *dukkha-dukkha-dukkha* about the *Ark*.

Notwithstanding its humble origins of stolen, fresh-cut trees and amateur labor, their boat seemed to embrace them more home-like than many cabins on the prairie. Here, feeling good, Abraham shined, easily engaging in conversations with Offutt.

He laughed to think it, but he won an argument already. Offutt, for all of his skills, was flummoxed every time he tried to raise a controversy or an argument about religion, the economy or even his usually-surefire issue of slavery. His most tried-and-true gambits failed with Abraham. Abraham told Offutt his secret: he had read the Constitution. He knew whereof he spoke.

"You do seem informed, although you are not educated," Offutt said, high praise from a man whose avocation for years, on horseback, on land, afloat, had been arguing. He was good at it, witty when not profane, profane when not witty, sharp-tongued and momentarily brilliant in turns. But Abraham's young mind stymied him. Their tussle would last as long as the trip, longer, truly. Taking it as a challenge, Offutt tried but could not wrestle Abraham into a stranglehold intellectually. He could not get a rise out of complacent, curious and honest Abraham. Before long, given Abraham's unexpected success, and Offutt's dilemma that Hanks would not talk, whether from his toothlessness and shyness or otherwise, his sole remaining victim was poor Johnny. Johnny afforded Offutt his chance to shine, of which Offutt took full and unfair advantage often and loudly, for all to savor with him.

"Johnny, does the sun rise and set or is it the earth that spins?" Offutt asked.

"I don't rightly know."

"Give it any thought?"

"No."

"Why not?"

"I don't know."

"You don't know why you don't give it any thought?"

"I figure it's not my business, the sun will do whatever it wants and so will the earth."

Offutt laughed and laughed. He would regularly repeat Johnny's answer as a sort of witticism. Even Abraham could not resist grinning at that. The fact that tickled was that Johnny had no more wit than a carrot.

CHAPTER TWENTY-TWO

The next day drifting, Abraham and Offutt stood together at the bow, watchful of the river but seeing only two painted turtles sunning themselves on a log harmlessly floating fifty yards away.

Unbidden, Abraham began, "There was this sick man in Illinois whose doctor told him to put his affairs in order, the end being near. Immediately, he had the minister come over and pray with him and the preacher said he ought to use his remaining time by making peace with any enemies. Now, it just happened that this man truly had only one enemy in all the world, a neighbor named Brown with whom he had a grudge over a hog each man had claimed and argued over with great insults and indignation some years previous. Brown, being sent for, appeared at the ailing fellow's bedside.

"'I wish to shake your hand,' the man told Brown in a voice as meek and mild as Jesus.

"They shook hands and Brown was so moved that he cried, then they both cried a regular love-feast of forgiveness broke out for a long visit.

"Come time to leave finally, it being hard for Brown to tear himself away from his newly befriended neighbor, they parted with embraces and words that would have melted the heart of a grindstone.

"Then, just as Brown reached the door, the sick man rose up on his elbow and called out, 'But, see here, Brown, one thing: if I should happen to get well, the old grudge stands.'"

Offutt laughed almost as heartily as Abraham did at his own joke, told one in turn, and then Abraham spun a very droll traditional fable involving The Trickster Fox and a chief's daughter. Offutt then decided to see if politics would bring Abraham out of his corner. Maybe he could pin him with a political issue.

"I figure you for a Jackson man," Offutt said as his opening.

"Did Hanks tell you so?" Abraham asked.

"He did not. But you are a settler in the west and a farmer among farmers, you seem likely to be a Jackson man."

"I defend him against slander," Abraham said. "I don't believe in personal abuse in politics. Editors who tell lies about Jackson make my stomach turn."

"Of his wife, more than of him," Offutt said.

"All the worse. Do not make me stand up to you, for I will, if you should take on much more in that direction."

"Is it dishonorable to raise a question that is plain from the face of public records? Answer me that question, Lincoln."

Jackson had obtained a divorce decree in court but then failed to follow through. It ought to have been passed by the legislature in order for him to remarry. For a time Jackson was technically a bigamist. Abraham stood among the many to whom this was nobody's business now. He confronted Offutt.

"The relation between a man and his wife is sacred. There exists no worse fiend than the man who ponders old records to find a flaw in dates or sequence or authority, as that with which they bedeviled poor Jackson and his wife."

Offutt was impressed by the felicitous fluency of his boatman.

"I say no more. I thought that you were a Jackson man," Offutt said.

"I'm an Adams man," Abraham now admitted. "But fairness to all is my motto."

"Too bad. I'm partial to our next President," Offutt said.

"And just who is that to be, Mr. Offutt?" Abraham asked, smiling. He would be able to vote next election. It would be his business, too, not just Offutt's.

"Henry Clay," Offutt said.

"Good man, could be," Abraham said of the Kentuckian who was both a slave owner and served as the head of a group that was freeing slaves and sending them back to Africa. Clay, with his neatly balanced views, was Abraham's *beau ideal* of a statesman but Abraham preferred John Quincy Adams, the educated son of a Founder who, while no abolitionist, would likely aim for changes. For all that, Abraham thought that Clay and Adams would both have to wait, along with any other Presidential hopefuls. Abraham thought that Jackson would be President for a good long time yet, for three or four terms if he wanted so many. In keeping with a policy of harmony, however, Abraham rested with his remark, "Good man, could be."

With that, despite differing views, both Offutt and Abraham were satisfied by their political talk.

CHAPTER TWENTY-THREE

Caleb Carman spotted the flatboat's imminent danger, which was his danger as well. Caleb, the biggest man in New Salem, worked in the grist mill at the end of the dam. He opened and yelled from his window in vain. No matter how loudly he shouted, "Boat! Boat! Watch the dam! Dam ahead of you!" nobody aboard heard him over the constant shhhhing noise of dam spillage. Caleb was thus the horrified, not-so-distant only witness as the *Ark* struck the New Salem dam.

When the flatboat caught on the lip of John Rutledge's milldam, Offutt rose from the top deck upon which he had been snoozing, took one look, saw water coming in, albeit slowly, at the stern end, lower as it was in the water, and began to sing:

Mortals, awake, with angels join
And chant the solemn lay;
Joy, love, and gratitude combine
To hail th' auspicious day

He then broke off. Johnny, Hanks and Abraham had already come forward and gone back down into the boat, where they were scrambling to grab and haul up anything they could. Some of the boat's cargo had best be unloaded in haste. Maybe the live hogs could stay. Offutt's help was to state what all three knew and were acting upon already.

"Here's what we do, boys, we unload what we can. With less weight, we'll pass up over the bar easy," Offutt announced.

What Caleb had feared most did not occur: the dam did not collapse; instead, however, the flatboat was pushed by current up onto the dam. This in turn led to the stern being at level with the stream. In a while, in an accelerating disaster, the flatboat would gradually fill with water and sink.

Nothing if not resourceful and quick-thinking, Caleb poled over to the flatboat in his large skiff. As he stood by, given their own ingenuity and Offutt's instructions, the crew worked hard. They quickly but carefully piled one balanced load for a first trip to shore, then another and another until, with Caleb's assistance, about half of Offutt's goods were safe. In two hours, barrels of apples, pork, potatoes in burlap sacks, all of the large, heavy sacks of flour, most of the tied bolts of cloth, folded quilts and blankets, cordage, buckets and brooms, boxes of shoes, boots, baby clothes, laces, a wooden box of percussion caps with red paint DANGER, two crates of patent medicines, a dental kit, musical instruments, candles, and dozens of tin mirrors printed with Offutt's name and lettering about his enterprises, with several animal traps, lined the shore under the steep embankment to New Salem village.

The crew's pantry barrels of sauerkraut, sacks of onions and carrots, a large barrel of buckwheat flour they also had Caleb move, not to be washed away. Nobody took so much care with Abraham's jew's harp, which Johnny almost "accidentally" tossed overboard but Abraham was too quick for him by a grab. Abraham thereafter kept it in his pocket.

As Caleb watched over the barrels and sacks and boxes piled on the shore, he was joined by another, a man in a shabby top hat and black jacket too small from him, an Irishman perhaps, a leprechaun, who now shouted:

"Halloo, do you need help?"

"We do," Offutt shouted between cupped hands.

"Do we?" Hanks asked, not much above a whisper.

"I like an audience," Offutt said back in an equal near-whisper.

"I'll get more help," the man said back, a fishing pole now up over his shoulder and a string of fish jiggling as he scampered uphill.

"Must be some people up there," Offutt said.

"Where there's a mill, there will be people," Hanks said.

Even unloaded to this extent, the boat remained precariously on the lip of the dam. The three men bailed furiously at the stern but it was still touch-and-go. Water spilled up and over the back of the boat. It could still founder before their trip had hardly begun. Tempers frayed, everybody was sensitive.

Standing atop the deck, holding to the flag pole, Offutt said, gesturing with a sweep of his free hand, "Have to get the hogs off, too, Hanks."

"Can't," Hanks said. He was smoking a small cigar that he clenched between his teeth. Seeing the man puffing away in front of him and talking as if he knew better set Offutt to yelling in a voice quite audible to folks on shore.

"Why 'can't'? You – you – you are always in the way, Hanks," Offutt said, just barely resisting the temptation to call Hanks something insulting. Grabbing his own hat, throwing it down and stamping on it, Offutt went on, "Always, always, always."

Hanks waited, then asked Offutt: "You want the truth or you want to pout more first?"

"Why 'can't'? That's all I want to know. You said it, Hanks, you prove it. That's the way it works. I'm in favor of progress, of getting along down this river, of getting off this bar and I'd welcome your cooperation. And any wisdom you care to share. Now, I'll pick up my hat here, brush it off," Offutt said, picking up his hast and brushing it off while he pumped it back into shape and then placed it carefully, like some precious crown atop his head. He finished by looking at Hanks and asking, "And you talk and remonstrate to me what you know. Why 'can't'?"

"Hogs get scared. You can't herd hogs like sheep or cattle. They get a-scared," Hanks said.

"That true, Abe?" Offutt asked.

"Why don't you ask me?" Johnny asked.

Lincoln nodded.

"Well, hogs, mules and butterflies are all alike hard to herd, Mr. Offutt," Abraham said, looking down to avoid smiling or laughing. Truth was truth.

The great pioneer and idea-generator, planner and future self-anointed emporium emperor of several states, Denton Offutt I said, the wood was burning hot under his hat, ""Tell you what we do is – we sew their eyes shut."

"What?" Hanks said, his jaw falling and his cigar dropping out of his mouth.

"What say, Hanks? 'Can't' again? Never tried, have you? Never tried to herd hogs with their eyes shut, have you? Why, the plan states itself. Most gentle to the hogs, no beating, no bruising. You can lead a blind pig because they want leading. They will follow."

"I don't know," Hanks said.

"Don't know until you try, Hanks. Let's get started, boys. The day is wasting, the ship is sinking. Where's needles and thread? Two, Johnny and Hanks, hold the hogs while the other two, Abe and me, do the sewing. Get this done and everybody gets a silver dollar extra down New Orleans."

"Praise Jesus," Johnny said.

Offutt sang as they scrambled now to sew hogs' eyes shut:

While sorrows encompass me round
And endless distresses I see,
Astonished I cry, can mortal be found
Surrounded with troubles like me?

CHAPTER TWENTY-FOUR

Within fifteen minutes a group formed on shore, lining along the beach, a handful, then doubling, then doubling again, hollering, "Come ashore," and "Over here."

That idea was impractical. The flatboat teetered on the dam and its crew had no way to move the boat anywhere else.

The well-intended villagers were curious, not self-interested, Offutt was certain. It did no harm to give them incentives not to steal, however. Assuming a benevolent role, Offutt shouted from his boat.

"Good people," he said, his arms wide in embrace. "I am a trader. I shall offer fair trades with you. Have you whiskey? fur and hides? Go home and find something to offer me. What I have in turn are marvels from all over, the like of which you miss if you miss trading with Denton Offutt today."

Abraham's jaw dropped, although he kept his mouth closed in a suppressed smile. Who else, standing upon a boat teetering on a dam and sinking, would make such a speech?

The narrow dam scarcely offered any footing, and an inch or two of water spilled over all along its length. Hanks studied it, casting his eye from where they were on over to shore. Then, he tossed his cigar, left the boat and trotted over the bar.

It was an awesome and unforgettable sight for all aboard and those ashore.

Goat-like balanced despite the flow of water as he walked, Hanks seemed for all the world like one walking on water. Upon reaching the bank, breathless, with its crowd of spectators, Hanks was specific about one thing. Hanks announced, "We are in urgent need of needles and strong thread or string. Anybody able to help us out?"

Of the crowd, a girl in front raised her hand. Nothing fancy about her, in a worn homespun dress and half-bonnet — it only partly covered a glorious head of auburn curls – she said, "I have some."

Aboard the *Ark*, Abraham's dog, Tiger, who had sat the entire trip quietly even up to the bump against the dam and as the boat listed, its prow rising, began now to bark.

"I have some in my basket," she said. Caught and called for the emergency while sewing, Ann Rutledge had not set down her sewing basket but brought it out with her.

Meanwhile, Offutt shouted from the flatboat, while pointing at two muscular, athletic types standing in the crowd, "You two, knock together a little holding pen. A hog apiece for each of you."

The two vanished, going for tools and split rails. Tiger continued barking, wagging his tail, running back and forth.

Offutt likewise begged aloud to borrow a boat.

"What for?" someone shouted back.

"For hogs," Offutt said.

"All right. Use our raft."

After another ten minutes, from shadows upstream, two men, brothers, worked to pole over a rectangular raft with wooden fencing and canvas flaps. Excitement spread like a contagion in the sleepy village of New Salem. The raft's owner and his brother would now share in the celebrity that was being generated by the incident.

"May I borrow the basket, ma'am?" Hanks asked the lady with the sewing basket, his hand out to receive it.

Aboard the flatboat, Abraham hushed Tiger to no avail. The dog continued to bark.

Ann passed it to Hanks, saying, "I also offer to take care of your dog until the danger's past."

Tiger howled.

"Kind of you, ma'am. He's not my dog but I think it will be appreciated by my young, handsome cousin, Abraham," Hanks said.

Hanks moved fast with the basket and told Abraham about the lady's offer.

Abraham hollered thanks, his hat off. Then he bent down and whispered into Tiger's ear, "Off you go now, follow the lady."

Tiger leaped off the flatboat into the water with a great splash and doggy-paddled his way to shore. Shaking off the wet, he scattered the crowd, even the lady, who ran off a few steps before returning. After that, Tiger was already following, leaping up at her heels, but stopping whenever she stopped. She laughed to see it. To Abraham, listening close aboard his sinking craft, that laugh was as the sound of temple bells and her face seemed radiant.

"Whose dog is he?" she asked.

"Abraham Lincoln," the tall man said, putting his hat on and then taking it off, adding, "m'am."

"Who owns the basket?" Hanks asked.

She said, "Ann Rutledge, sir."

Within minutes, Offutt sat tailor-like on the deck, his legs crossed, as he squinted at Ann Rutledge's open basket and gingerly selected needles and then, with prissy diffidence, took up spools of coarse black thread for himself and

Abraham. Abraham volunteered to join Offutt in the experiment. It was just the type of unprecedented project that made him thrill to be alive. Not that he had much tailoring or surgeon experience.

"Done much sewing?" Offutt asked Abraham.

"Darned my own socks."

"Me, too. Hog's eyes will be new to both of us."

Offutt assigned Hanks and Johnny the task of holding the hogs while they sewed their eyes shut.

"She was pretty," Hanks said to Abraham.

"Didn't notice," Abraham said.

"Oh, I saw you."

"Then you must have eyes in back of your head," Abraham said.

"You used to be more honest, cuz."

"I didn't say she wasn't pretty, I just said I didn't notice. Meaning that I did not take official note or render judgment," Abraham said.

"Ain't you the politician?"

"I do not deny any particular ambition. All men have their ambitions, and a poor boy may not be so fussy as a rich one."

"And you also did not deny looking, just said I must have eyes in back of my head. I know your tricks. You could make a lawyer," Hanks said, as Abraham sewed the squealing pig.

"Hold tighter, Johnny, grab his legs there, both of them," Hanks told Johnny.

"He's shitting," Johnny said.

"More where that came from, just hold," Hanks said.

"It's slippery," Johnny said, murmuring "oooh" at the stink of it.

"Hold tight, Johnny. Squirming will spoil the surgery," Abraham said, very fast with his sewing.

"You done with this one yet?" Johnny whined.

"Done," Abraham said, having cut and tied off his handiwork. "Next hog."

Hanks placed the now-blind hog down, who ran in panic and hit the wall, fell and then ran in further circles. This ludicrous result continued to be repeated as each hog was temporarily blinded, although not without a great deal of defecation by each in mute protest against such treatment. By the time they were through on the flatboat, the two men ashore had knocked together a holding pen on the sandy bank of the river, small but suitable for the hogs. The flatboat men, who stank as bad as the pigs now, covered as they were with dirt and defecation, were more than willing to drive the hogs — if they could.

CHAPTER TWENTY-FIVE

That afternoon and evening New Salem opened its homes to the travelers. Everybody wanted to meet, watch and talk with the strangers. Passersby were always welcome diversions in the cluster of cabins ten miles from Petersburg. But these passersby had arrived under striking circumstances, defying sinking, rich with goods in an amount they rarely saw, even at a merchant's. They sought to talk, to trade, to learn from these men. Of them all, Abraham had the least to say and Johnny, even ahead of Offutt, the most. Johnny was full of brags and questions and opinions. Only Hanks was almost as quiet as Abraham, but they got him talking about the future of Illinois and then he was off and running. Those of this village had hopes but nothing more yet besides a mill, one store and a tavern. The mill and tavern were John Rutledge's and it was where Ann lived with her family. It was to the tavern that Abraham went with Tiger, who ran on ahead as if to insist.

Offutt pulled John Rutledge aside and then, after a few words of huddled conference, asked Hanks to join him in a "walk out to the mill." He was going to talk business, Abraham thiought, and he wanted a witness to any handshake deal. Abraham and Johnny stayed, but they did not stay together long. A few of the men were interested in a game of quoits and Johnny was up for the fun. He peeled away with them, leaving Abraham in the Rutledge tavern alone for a time. Where was Mrs. Rutledge or Ann? Perhaps upstairs. It was strange that the tavern was left to him and Tiger. The hubbub over quoits outside brought everyone from any cabin to attend until a good thirty or forty stood outside on the green.

After some ten minutes — Johnny having displayed no great shakes at quoits after all — the crowd, getting both bored and thirsty, moved inside the tavern, led by a cadaverous man with deep set eyes. They were deeper set than any eyes Abraham could recall, ending in an electrifyingly icy-blue pair of eyes when he lifted his head up to give them a view — who walked in rather stiffly but all the same presented a striking figure. Although close-shaven of face, his hair was all gorgon-like atop his head, not having seen a comb in days, if then. It turned out that he rarely combed or cut, just ran his fingers up in the course of the day once or twice.

Despite or perhaps because of the hush inside the tavern, it ran through Abraham's mind that this was a corpse returning to life. Then, in a soft, nearly feminine voice, in a drawl as soft and evocative as a Kentucky native but presenting the immediately obvious vocabulary of a traveled man, the strange man said, "Welcome, traveler from afar, to this humble village of ours. All the blessings of this place need you take upon the resumption of your journey southward. Whither art thee bound?"

Abraham had thought that Allen Gentry sounded educated and impressive but this man, Abraham now thought, this apparent spokesman for the men and women here, was possibly a wizard who spoke Latin and could spell standard English. To find such a man in this village was a surprise to him yet, he counseled himself, a body must be somewhere. Could he tell that joke with effect here tonight?

"Abraham Lincoln, sir," he said, stretching out his hand and feeling conscious of its calluses. "Who might you be?"

"Mentor Graham," the unblinking man said, shaking, coming near as if to take in Abraham's face and future in a long, close sustained scrutiny.

"Tell him how you saw the dam commenced," a voice said, not unkindly but with a curl of a rub to the question.

"I did see the dam commenced," Mentor said sharply. "I don't know that Mr. Lincoln wishes to hear about that."

"I do, Mr. Graham," Abraham said, his eyes intent upon this teacher. Graham launched himself with, "It was legislatively chartered in order to be built. It is the largest public work, accomplished by private hands, in the history of this county."

Big Caleb Carman feared a long and dry description of the days of preparation, the design and the length of the dam. He, and all of them except Abraham, had heard it all before.

"Excuse me, Mentor. Let me introduce Abraham around now," Caleb said, taking Abraham up from his bench to be introduced to a physician, Dr. Duncan, a graduate of Yale University, a former lawyer, and to a handful of other literate folk. Dr. Duncan said that he was "by good fortune the most educated member of the community, next after Mentor" and mentioned that he'd have been first except that he had "not seen the dam commenced." Abraham gleaned that the dam story was Mentor's one monomania.

"This one is our fisherman, Jack Kelso," Caleb said, bringing forward a diminutive and shabby man with a turned-up nose. Abraham recognized his face and slight figure.

"How do," Kelso said, as Abraham shook his hand.

Abraham asked Kelso if it was not he who had spread the word about the flatboat's peril and Kelso said that it was, whereupon Abraham slapped his back, hugged him and thanked him in two words just as he would have at home.

"I'd say something appropriate but I'm no speaker," Abraham said, drawing the laugh.

Kelso recited some lines of poetry, which was lost in the buzz of voices asking and telling about the day and the doings of the village.

"Do you recite?" Abraham asked, recognizing in Kelso a kindred spirit.

Kelso said that he not only recited, he debated.

"Saturdays in this very establishment in which you stand, sir, the voice of Jack Kelso is raised with the demonstration of himself as instrument of wisdom, and there are those here present who can vouch for this as my witnesses."

Around him, some murmured assent and others laughed. Abraham took him for both a prickly and a popular character, one needed to bring spice to the life of a village, one such as he longed for on his isolated farm in Indiana and, now, in Illinois. A weekly meeting at which philosophical questions were debated sounded like a dream, as close to paradise as Abraham might ever reach, and this was going on in New Salem, under this roof. So near and yet so far.

Here, in this tiny site of earth, lived thought. Thinking people gave hours to reading, to writing and to speaking. Nobody failed to sow, to weed, to hoe, to harvest. They made shoes, climbed up ladders to repair roofs, fixed their chimneys, redid chairs. They made a world that, in his isolated cabin, he only dreamed of.

In the Rutledge tavern, ladies now appeared, coming so lightly downstairs that none heard their tread. Invited to sit by Ann's mother, Abraham was in no position to restrain Tiger, who nuzzled Ann, who laughed.

"I am a student of Mr. Graham's," Ann said, her first words to Abraham ashore. Thus she introduced herself as a learner, not as learned. Her claim was modest. Had Abraham thought about it, the remark would have pleased Abraham but instead he stared, thinking that Ann's eyes were wider than out on the river when they'd first met at a distance, before any words. Maybe it was a trick of the candlelight in the cabin, though, where at least a dozen candles were burning in an extravagant glow that made it seem like dazzling day. Not like the Lincolns' cabin. Hadn't it snowed here in New Salem?

"What do you study?" Abraham asked.

"Well, for one thing, voice. I am studying to sing. I bring Watt's Hymns over to his cottage and first he sings me a sample and then next I try and do my best."

Abraham squirmed and tried to find a comfortable position on his chair but could not. Singing was not his strength.

"Mentor says I am getting better. He wants to learn me grammar, too, and spelling. I can write but I don't practice so much as I should."

This Mentor Graham had it over him in Ann's eyes, Abraham could see. He felt his eyes get slopey, as they did whenever he felt sad.

"You write letters," her little sister said, who had been caressing Tiger and giving his forehead little kisses.

"You hush up," Ann said, with a surprising harsh tone he'd not observed earlier. She had a temper and could show it.

"You write letters?" Abraham asked.

Ann blushed.

"I write but I get no replies is what," Ann said, leaning near him and lowering her voice. "A gentleman that used to live here, named John McNamar, that's who I write to. Some letters come back, others don't but I never hear back from him."

"In how long?" Abraham asked.

"Two years," Ann said.

"She's always going to the store to see if there is a letter," the little girl said.

"Now, you — hush," she told her, pointing this time. "Shall I ask Maw to give you a spank?"

The little one turned and ran off.

"Well," Abraham said. "Well."

"Yes," Ann said. "It is well. I may as well say it myself. It is well that I hear no more from that man."

"Yes," Abraham said. So Mentor Graham was not the rival that he need be concerned with, but this man McNamar. But McNamar? He seemed to have, as they say in the military, retired from the field.

James Rutledge, Ann's tall father, came back into the tavern, throwing some outside.

"Make room," he said, calling them by name, and they obeyed. Abraham noted it. James Rutledge was not a man of many words but what he said, stood.

James hauled Offutt and Hanks into the place and hollered for his wife to bring something to drink to "the gentlemen."

Abraham imagined that Offutt had probably cooked up a deal of some kind, which later proved to be correct.

James Rutledge, spying Abraham, came striding over, and shook hands with a good, strong grip.

"James Rutledge, founder of New Salem, and the engineer of its great dam, sir. I like you, Abram," Rutledge said.

Ann said, "Abraham is his name, Paw. Ain't it?"

She turned to Abraham.

"I am Abraham Lincoln. Some call me Abe or Abram. I don't mind."

"I'm going to call you by your name, and it's Ab-ra-ham," Ann said.

Her father nodded and, without more to say, left altogether, his fine leather boots making a racket on the floorboards — everything so much grander and more stylish than in his cabin, where Pa walked about slow and crawly in stockings — Ann took him by the elbow and all but whispered, "I'm going to write a letter to you, Abraham, and it will be waiting for you in New Orleans, so best remember. Check at the post office."

Abraham was certain that any letter would be carried faster and would arrived in New Orleans far ahead of the flatboat.

"Are you sure?" Abraham asked, mulling over a gal writing him so soon after writing this McNamar.

CHAPTER TWENTY-SIX

Mentor Graham, after a last sip of cider, held up his hand.

"Ladies and gentlemen, and children," Mentor said, his hand sweeping magician-like and simultaneously creating silence in the tavern.

He then asked, "Has our guest any tale to tell us? Would a tale satisfy the reckoning, James?"

James bellowed, "Depends on the story."

They all laughed.

"Mr. Abraham Lincoln, if you will rise and give us what you care by way of entertainment, we will be beholden and much in your debt, sir."

Abraham stood and spent no time looking at the floor or wondering where his hands ought to be, in his pockets or free. With a smile and a glance at Ann for courage, he started up with the story.

"Seems there was this boy, Rastus, down to Kentucky who had more of an appetite for chicken than he had chicken.

"He had fast fingers, though."

He made his fingers wriggle as if feeling up under a loose board or under a wire fence. The audience laughed. Abraham went on.

"So, one night, the farmer in bed at his cabin by the hen-house," here Abraham made a fist and rubbed his nose while he crinkled his eyes, saying, "you married men know about being in bed but awake."

The ribaldry sufficed for a good laugh from all, not only men. The children joined, not from knowing what was funny but from sheerly wanting to join in.

"Well, anyhow, all of a sudden there came such a commotion and noise from that hen-house that he came quickly to the con-clusion," Abraham said, pausing, which led to renewed laughter, "that something was wrong and he'd best get on his boots, get his shotgun and sashay outside to investigate.

"So he did.

"He stood at the hen-house door and yelled, 'I'm outside with my shotgun and I'm telling you all inside to get up and out of there.'

"Inside, Rastus yelled back, 'Oh, massa, ain't nobody in here but us chickens.'"

Ann was the one whose face he watched with great pleasure as she, although covering her mouth lady-like with both hands, otherwise laughed freely.

"Have you got just one more for us, Abraham?" Mentor asked.

Abraham looked at Ann, who was all eyes now.

"Well, maybe just this one more, Mentor," he said. But one more led to another until, that evening, Abraham had them in gales of laughter frequently. Offutt and Hanks came straggling into the tavern and asked Abraham to help with reloading, so off he went, but already a hero. John Rutledge led in a toast "To the crew and captain."

Offutt said, in turn, "To all of our new friends in New Salem."

After sipping and saying ahhh, Offutt added, "Why, in common with the great Shakespeare, of our accident I declare that 'the tears live in an onion that should water this sorrow.'"

An approving, admiring murmur went around the room, "He knows Shakespeare." Although invited, none of them slept in the village that night. They spent time bailing the Ark until it floated. All night in rotation, one would bail while the others slept. Water kept sloshing over the stern. They had not removed enough cargo to float above the surface of the Sangamon. But, with bailing, they were not going under. An absence of windows had helped.

"You like that the boat has no window, after all, Johnny?" Hanks asked, teasing him.

Johnny would not say anything. He knew that the air-tight boat had survived its collision with the dam in part because it had no windows.

He took first shift bailing.

The rest fell asleep, Offutt under a blanket on the top deck, Hanks and Abraham in their damp bed-shelves. Their homemade *Ark of the Covenant* just might make it down the Mississippi. The boat that they all wrested out from under the people of the United States floated. What had been trees standing on the river bank but a month and a half earlier would be reloaded and relaunched the next day.

CHAPTER TWENTY-SEVEN

By mid-morning the next day, the *Ark* lay idle past the dam. It had been no small feat. Working with poles as levers, prying with directions by Abraham, whose strength was key and with whose movements everyone else had to coordinate and synchronize, the boat had slipped up over the dam and then leaned slowly until it slid into the river below, all without damage to the dam or breaking up.

It had been a show closely observed by a wide-eyed crowd of about fifty. All of the villagers and some settlers from nearby outskirts, like Mentor Graham and his wife, milled about the banks. A couple seated on a boat, four young ones standing on a raft, too, on the river were, all of them, too, alive just to see the re-launching of the *Ark,* near shore and accessible from the shore via Caleb's anchored skiff, functioning like a bridge.

The Ark was edged near to shore and rendered accessible from the shore via Caleb's anchored skiff, functioning like a bridge or magic carpet for cargo. The crowd stood open-mouthed appreciating the equally fascinating reloading (but for the hogs) as that unfolded next.

When that was over, for a time, before getting to the hogs, Abraham and Ann stood together at the edge of the excited shoreline crowd.

Only Kelso fished and concerned himself with anything other than the *Ark.*

Jack Kelso, the thoughtful-looking, short, young man in a broad-brimmed straw hat familiar to Abraham from the day before, was casting for fish in the river and not looking in the direction of Ann and Abraham.

"What's wrong with Jack?" Abraham whispered to Ann.

"Nothing. Jack's heart is always on fishing," she said in normal tones. Either Ann was not good at whispering or she knew that Jack would not take offense were he to hear her.

Kelso did not look toward them, still held his view on the river.

"Fishing?" Abraham asked, himself in normal tones now.

"Don't mind him. He's a fisherman and never thinks about anything but fishing."

Offutt shook hands with Rutledge, in front of Hanks as witness, over renting the Rutledge mill and, as part of the deal, Rutledge storing some of the cargo for a store that Rutledge would build that spring for occupancy by Offutt by August. It was all on credit and conditional upon Offutt's surviving and returning from New Orleans. Rutledge had long hoped against hope that New Salem would expand as one of the state's cities. He was well aware that this required commerce, commerce that required connections, and connectors like dynamic Offutt. Rutledge noted how popular Offutt was with everybody, and such a gift could be just what New Salem needed. He hated to part with his quite profitable grist mill even for a season, but if that was what it took to anchor Offutt to the village, Rutledge gladly made that sacrifice.

The *Ark* was about to resume its interrupted journey.

The hogs remained.

What would Offutt do?

The business of the hogs, although it had done nothing to add luster to the image of the crew as heroic, had stoked up interest and awareness all around. Offutt's name was now known in half of the county. The story spread as a fabulous tale, along with excitement over what would follow. It was a tale told emphasizing that Offutt's plan had gone perfectly up through the sewing the eyes. Laughter then began with describing how, thereafter, the panicked, blind hogs could not be herded, held, calmed or placed anywhere. People who had not seen the fun made merry over the chase, hearing how the hogs ran through the woods and village of New Salem. Its residents had become an unsworn hog posse, engaged in the new sport of blind hog catching, working in teams, using poles, nets and other devices. The round up by Offutt and his crew and many volunteers was celebrated.

Now, the fifty or so people — more than for the biggest wedding — wanted to see, if not to help and play walk-on roles in the drama of the *Ark* being loaded with the hogs.

Hanks gave the basket back to Ann.

"Do you mind if we borrow small scissors and thread hooks a while longer?" Hanks asked Ann. He explained that they would need to snip the pigs' shut eyes.

"You'll give everything back, though?" Ann asked in an anxious tone. New Salem was not a town but an isolated village where every rare sewing needle or thread-hook made a long journey before getting into their hands. And Hanks, after all, despite his appearance as an honest man, was a stranger.

Hanks said that he would be personally responsible. He said, "Just give us an hour."

Ann then asked Abraham if he would like her to keep Tiger. She understood risks on the river. When Abraham looked at Tiger, he stood begging, his paws in the air, and whining piteously.

"I think he'd like that more than to see New Orleans," Abraham said.

Abraham asked her if it would be all right that he would be back for the dog in the summer, after the Fourth of July.

"It's not going to be earlier than July," Abraham said.

Ann seemed to think belatedly of her father, and his possible objections.

"Does he hunt? My father could use a hunter," Ann said.

"I don't know if he's ever hunted," Abraham said.

"You don't hunt?" Ann asked, looking him in the eye.

He blushed.

"No, ma'am. I don't hunt. Sometimes I find but I don't hunt."

They both smiled at one another.

Ann repeated about writing. She said, "I will take care of him. And I will send you word of how your dog is doing. I shall write a letter and send it next week to New Orleans. Don't forget to inquire at its post office."

Abraham didn't know what to say in turn but noted that Offutt, who was catching the spirit of the day from the crowd, was now standing.

"Offutt's going to speak now," he said.

Why, Abraham wondered, was it so hard for him to part from his dog? As he clambered off without so much as an excuse me or farewell, Ann said goodbye. He did not look back but took the few steps across the raft and got up aboard the *Ark*.

"The boy don't know enough to say good-bye. No proper gentleman," a New Salem wife, Parthenia Hill, said to Ann.

"What I'd call a natural honest man," Ann said, her nose and chin up.

Parthenia said, "I didn't know you were so taken with him."

She was going to tattle and rattle about her engagement to McNamar, Ann thought.

"I'm just saying he's honest, he puts on no airs. No more than that, Parthenia Hill."

"I understand, gal. McNamar's honesty remains to be seen."

The village women were impatient with McNamar, even more than Ann herself.

The dog, at Ann's side, barked and barked.

Offutt did not speak. First, he had a miracle to perform.

The now-experienced surgeons, Offutt and Abraham, snipped and undid the sutures and made the blind see. A dozen people crowded aboard the raft beside the flatboat. The raft began to tip and they had to relent in their desire to see the operations. Only five or six could stand on the raft and see the hogs, giddy and exhausted, and hear close-up a chorus of ecstatic oinking noises as might greet a return of sight.

Only when the operations were over and Hanks had returned, in hand, Ann's scissors and thread hooks, was it time for his sermon.

Now, at last, Offutt was ready to address them. To overcome the roar of the falls, to be heard at all over the booming waters, Offutt had to go to full volume.

Unfurling and snapping a whip much as an impresario of the circus, Offutt announced, "Ladies and gentlemen, you have just witnessed two of the most extraordinary feats ever known on the Sangamo or any other river. You have just witnessed for yourself the blind see. In the past day, you saw first-hand for yourselves the precarious, nay, frightening and utterly life-jeopardizing predicament in which *The Ark of the New Covenant* stood.

"Thanks to the watchful God overhead who knows when even a sparrow falls, and thanks also to that ever-resourceful hero whom I am privileged to employ, Abraham Lincoln, we have saved the boat, the crew, the cargo — the benighted hogs — and all."

Offutt put a long burr on "ever-r-r-r-r-esourceful heeero" and, as he pronounced the name of the farmboy who had quickly become everybody's favorite, the crowd ashore cheered and applauded loudly. Offutt took a bow himself, to whoops.

"We depart now for New Orleans, the Crescent City. But we shall return."

This brought an ovation even greater: someone had seen New Salem and were still going to come back. Offutt waved to them with both hands outstretched, to stop their noises and give him a chance to conclude.

"Fair ladies and handsome gentlemen, and delightful children, I am going to build a noble steamboat to plow up and down the Sangamo, in all seasons, in flood and in drought, in summer and in winter. That vessel shall be well worth your seeing and guarantee your safe passage in riding upon her. She shall be outfitted with rollers to permit ready transit over shoals and dams, and be fitted in season with runners for ice. With young man Lincoln in charge as its captain, I daresay, we may cheer now as we shall next year, 'By thunder, but she shall go.'

"Thank you, one and all. Please remember the names of Denton Offutt and the intrepid and resourceful captain, Abraham Lincoln."

As the crowd huzzahed and gave three cheers, and the young fisherman at the side gave a wave and a nod, the flatboat uneventfully resumed its journey, its cargo reclaimed and odd whitewashed wooden sails in place. Offutt offered a spontaneous serenade over the water, singing to the New Salemites:

Alas! And did my Saviour bleed
And did my Sovereign die?
Would he devote that sacred head
For such a worm as I?

As the *Ark* drifted out into the middle of the Sangamon, the falls were more audible than Offutt's voice. Some only barely made out his words. Most only saw his mouth moving and heard no song. But, in its strangeness as an event, for those aboard the boat, with their first real audience receding and acclaim fading but yet in the air, Offutt's speech and singing cast a magic and a majesty about their travel.

Only one wrinkle rankled.

Offutt had named Abraham captain.

If anyone was to be dubbed captain, Hanks felt that he was entitled. Had not Offutt recruited Hanks first — the "experienced boatman" of the Ohio? Had Offutt not been so impressed that he had, single-handed, poled a fully loaded flatboat all across the Ohio safely? Where had Offutt's admiration gone? Had not Hanks led in the decision to build him this flatboat of which Abraham was suddenly captain?

Hanks did not talk with Offutt for two days.

CHAPTER TWENTY-EIGHT

About a half-mile downstream, the captain of the *Ark* spotted a portly gentle-man, cross between a merchant and a farmer to judge from his old top hat and his coveralls, who was waiting at bankside hailing the flatboat. Abraham asked Offutt if he ought to stop. Offutt said yes, keeping a sharp eye on him as Abraham hailed back "Coming ashore" and the man said, pointing, "Dock here." A sort of short pier stood fifty feet down a bend in the river.

"I may just," Offutt said, more to himself than to Abraham.

"What?" Abraham asked, seeing nothing untoward in a man with a herd of pigs being riverside and seeming ready to help them be loaded onto the flatboat from a pier.

"I spy that he has pigs in a corral at that pier. He must have heard news from New Salem of a hogger coming. But, I ask you, Abe — have I yet bought his pigs?"

"No," Abraham said, smiling, aware of a lesson coming as Offutt slid into the role of his teacher. Abraham loved to learn and had had little in his life to inspire it, three ignorant teachers, no more than one year altogether, schooling by littles. Abraham had learned to read, write, and to spell pretty much on his own. He still lacked grammar, good spelling and was conscious that gentlemen spoke differently and better than he did.

"Have we met on price?" Offutt asked.

"No," Abraham said.

"So we see a man on the bank, interested in getting rid of his many pigs, and a boat that can pass them by and either go without pigs or buy them else-where. Who would you say has the advantage, Abe?"

"You do, Mr. Offutt," Abraham said.

"I aim to get these pigs for twenty cents a head."

"That's half-price," Abraham said, turning things over in his head. "It's been a long winter. Pigs are not as common as last year."

"These, you see, are half-wild pigs. I shall remind that gentleman myself and loudly that they've scavenged, he did not feed them, he only caught them."

"He'll still want forty cents. Pigs is pigs, they say, you know. Pork is pork."

"And a man standing by the river with wild pigs he cannot wait to get rid of, wild pigs for which he paid nothing, whom we may pass by if we like, and then he will have to feed them or let them loose, well, that is what it is, too."

Abraham got to grinning at that and, calling to John Hanks, Hanks helped with a manful thrashing of water with his long oar in back as Abraham in the bow poled the boat in toward shore, gradually coming up to and tossing a line at the pier from about ten feet, a line the gent secured with alacrity.

"Morning, Squire," Offutt said. "You hailed us. We stopped. What can we do for you?"

The gent pursed his mouth, adopting a pout.

"Goodby's the name. Call me Squire if you like. It's not what you can do for me, it is what I can do for you. I can fill your cargo hold with these fine, healthy, young pigs, tender, good eating, victuals that will fetch a pretty penny in New Orleans."

"Well, we have three dozen hogs already aboard, but name your price, Goodby," Offutt said.

"Why, just because it's you, old friend, market price, no premium for delivery to your boat. I'll throw in my help loading."

"What is market?"

"Why, forty cents, of course."

"I appreciate, maybe you'd best bring these little, scrawny runts to market and fetch your forty cents a snout. I'd be lucky if any of these wild things survive the trip, and even then New Orleans is going to see wild pigs, all bone, no meat, no flavor."

"You know the market's forty cents."

"Maybe yesterday, maybe a sow with flesh, brought up on oats and barley. But these here are wild. You caught them, did you not?"

"I have corralled and fed them —"

"You caught them, and make no mistake, you can still turn them into coin right here, right now, I have the silver, ready money, twenty cents a head."

"Twenty —"

"Take it or leave it. I'm in haste. I already have corn and I have hogs. I cannot afford to be the last boat to New Orleans and this flatboat is not built for speed. What is your answer?"

Squire reddened and stammered.

"Done," Squire said. "But you owe me favor on future occasions of purchase or sale between us."

"That I do, Squire," Offutt said, nudging Abraham and whispering. "You see that he is already presenting himself as one of our customers and suppliers."

After Goodby helped with loading, it took little time before they were poling out to center stream again, to go with the current.

"The pigs were loaded quickly," Abraham said.

"The Squire was bested quicker," Offutt said. "I think I shall go above and enjoy a cigar."

And so Offutt did, puffing away beside the unadorned flagpole.

"Lincoln, we must get a big flag in Saint Louis," Offutt said.

CHAPTER TWENTY-NINE

As they floated down the Illinois River, Offutt showed how they ought to enter the cabin, which had no door but a green curtain hanging to separate their bunks from the cargo. At the same time, he practiced the few French words he knew, reminding them that French was the "*lingua franca*" of New Orleans.

"We don't want to bump into each other in the dark down here. So, *voilà*, we come up to the curtain and say, '*Regardez*,' and anybody in back of the curtain knows to expect somebody."

Offutt had them all practice saying '*Regardez*.'

Abraham recalled grammar school, when his teacher had them learn manners and etiquette, introducing one another, taking off caps and bowing.

Abraham, rocking in the flatboat but not restful as a babe in a cradle, some old trauma jostled awake in his mind, dreamed of wild eyes, slaves' eyes, he was sure, eyes in night, maybe clubs, smacking sounds, a nightmare feeling in his fast-beating heart.

Then he heard the Voice.

Blood coming.

He was scared fully awake. Thereupon, his mind wandered among his horrors. He saw his mother die again, and he was with his sister. Poor Sally. Now he was dreaming *Blood coming.* Was this journey south, too, fated for trouble? Sleep being impossible, Abraham dressed and went up the ladder to the top deck.

Johnny was at the front, the lamps were lit. Everything was all right.

"Can't sleep," Abraham said. "You want to turn in?"

"Glad to," Johnny said. As he passed his step brother, he patted his shoulder and said, "Thank 'ee."

"Nothing, brother," Abraham said. Abraham climbed down off the top deck, dropping into the bow and picking up a long oar just in case. They were lit up and any steamboat would be audible at a distance.

Questions came to him, especially on sleepless nights. Why had they no spiders aboard? When it was lightning over the river, he asked Offutt what lightning was. Offutt said something but Abraham, laughed out loud and cried, "You're stumped."

Offutt shrugged and spat back, "What you want to know about lightning for, anyways? You plan on going up in a balloon? Why not ask what the moon is made of then, in case you might ever walk on it? Abraham, you ask more

questions about nit-picking details of life than anybody I ever met, saw or over-
heard or heard of."

Abraham did not care. He was educating himself, one question at a time.
Offutt was not as good a teacher as Allen Gentry had been, but tuition was free
and way to New Orleans gave time. Here on the river was the school he never
had, the older brother, the wiser father, the learned man he otherwise never had
at home.

Abraham stood watch alone.

Johnny was something between alert and unconscious. He kept shaking
and startling, then slumping and resuming, embraced by a woman, a faceless
but comforting women. Hanks was in deep, dreamless sleep. Offutt dreamed
of a huge treasure chest filled with golden coins. How much wealth was just
within his grasp now. Anyone near his bunk with a lamp would have been able
to see his mouth curl into a smile.

CHAPTER THIRTY

They were in the Mississippi now, and its confluence with the muddy Missouri above St. Louis.

To shave and, better yet, to strip and bathe either with a wet washcloth dropped and hauled back up from the river soaking. Given half a chance, they all seized an opportunity whenever it came to clean up. It made them feel better for days to be facially hairless and less grubby. They could even use a bit of soap and scrub their clothes, which dried on their back quick enough. Their noses were then reborn and everything near smelled sweet, although at an arm's length the smell of their piggery was indelible.

Hanks and Johnny jumped into the river, swimming a bit and climbing back aboard one of the side-ropes, but not Offutt, who preferred something solid under his feet, smoking his cigar and watching from the upper deck, and not Abraham.

"Why'n't you swim, Abe?" Johnny asked one time early on, swimming about himself and floating.

"Gators," Abraham said.

Johnny turned from floater to swimmer in a flash, shouting, "You see one?"

"No," Abraham said.

Johnny stayed then, treading water but looking all around.

"You still spoiled it for me, Abe," he said.

"Just answered what you asked. I'm ascared of gators. I'll tell you why if you want to know."

Back aboard and after getting dressed, sitting to dry in the sun, Johnny asked Abraham what was the story about gators. Abraham said it was somebody he saw the first trip he made down the river.

CHAPTER THIRTY-ONE

It had been three years but Abraham instantly recognized St. Louis and he alone among them on the flatboat could tell them where the boat ought to aim and the side of the city that they'd be best served to head toward after they landed. That Abraham felt partial toward St. Louis followed logically. This city had never done him harm. Here, he had felt at home. It was the largest city he had ever seen up to when he first saw it, and he never forgot having been offered a job cutting wood at good wages.

St. Louis was a city of a thousand boats, it seemed, certainly with hundreds of flatboats moored or anchored or tied criss-cross to piers jutting wildly out into the river. On Militia Day, it was a perfect madhouse.

Now, for the first time, Abraham thought that a figure he read once might be true: that 3,000 flatboats went down the Mississippi each year. Their boat, the *Ark of the Covenant*, as large as it had seemed on its launch day on the Sangamon, was but bringing up the rear of that great flotilla.

Offutt had only intended a quick stop for provisions, getting some dry hard-tack and barrels of water loaded on by slaves. However, happening upon Saint Louis on its annual muster tempted him to decide to stay overnight. As everywhere else, in Saint Louis, Militia Day broke down eventually into a wild carnival of shooting and athletics. Fueled by consumption of alcohol, men eighteen to forty-five momentarily freed from their farms were out to shout. The illusion of patriotism elevated the activity into a law-mandated happy day, their one holiday. Who was so niggardly that he would not treat the boys to a round of libations?

The annual muster of the state militia companies and the United States Army brigade was a raucous and colorful time.

"First time seeing soldiers?" Offutt asked all aboard.

"I *am* a soldier, with the Spies," Hanks said with a certain sourness. Hanks was, after all, planning to depart for home now from St. Louis.

"After the war, we had soldiers over to our house and fed them back in Indiana," Abraham reminisced. Abraham was referring to the last war, against Great Britain, from 1812 to 1815. Abraham, seven or eight, had given his day's catch, a string of fish, to a passing soldier. Pa had said to be good to soldiers.

Those comments left only Johnny, who mumbled that he had never seen any soldiers.

Offutt went to see about a wagon to transport them and some of their cargo to trade.

Upon returning in a small wagon, he had obviously already done some trading. Standing precariously atop a sack of flour under one foot and a barrel of water under the other, Offutt yelled as he came near the *Ark*, "Soldier boys, all disembark."

Offutt had also brought along a guard with a weapon that resembled a blunderbuss to stay aboard and watch the cargo and the flatboat.

"This is like no boat I ever saw," the guard said, a lad of no more than fifteen. He jabbered on when aboard, touching the wooden sails. "I never seed such sails as these."

"Don't go on about the boat, lad," Offutt said. "Go on about your business. Stand up on deck."

The boy stood as if at attention.

"I am counting on you and I know your face and your name and I will send these men after you if you don't keep careful watch. I expect to return to find nothing missing."

"Yes, sir," the boy said.

The yard itself have two or three guards in patrol, a group of thugs not completely trusted. They were to respond to calls for help, fires or gunshots. They were thought to be capable of stealing themselves but the Offutt flatboat was no likely target and, in any case, the word was that the patrol got a cut when one paid an individual guard, even a boy. They then shadowed all of the boats with guards.

It had been hard to find a guard on Militia Day, when all not in the militia wanted to watch the militia drill, and then all wanted to imbibe.

They filled the cart with themselves after they unloaded the sack of flour and barrel of water.

"All right, driver," Offutt said as their cart drew them off to the parade ground.

They saw the militia. They smelled the barbecue, six sides of oxen and unlimited hog pieces and parts, roasted and fried. Smoke rose up to the god of all wars, filling his nostrils with these sacrifices. None of them missed his chance to gnaw a bone clean, wiping dripping juice off their faces with linen tear-cloths in innumerable baskets carried about by slave women and children. Here and there a few of the ladies, young and many not so young, were smiling at likely men who might come to them and converse. Men and women got together at musters as often as at revival meetings.

At one parade, Offutt stood beside Hanks.

"Ain't it a stirring sight? Listen to the drums and fifes," Offutt said.

"Grand day," Hanks said.

"So many sights you'll miss if you leave us here," Offutt said.

"I promised my wife, Mr. Offutt," Hanks said.

"Denny, Hanks, call me Denny. I was there. I heard your words, they were given on account of her fear of hazard," Offutt said.

"Yes."

"Is it not more hazardous for one man to travel than four?"

"I don't know about that, Denny. Depends on who the four are."

"You, your two cousins Abraham and Johnny, and Denny Offutt."

"But it's still on a boat, Denny. On the river."

"Hanks, she expected you to be on a boat built by strangers, an old boat. Not a new one built by your own good and capable hands."

"That's true, Denny."

"If she were here and knew that you could continue your trip more safely than walking back home to her alone, with twice the money ahead of you, is that not acceptable?"

"If I had not promised her, Denny. Did you say twice the money?"

"Hanks, if you complete this trip. Twice the money, Hanks."

"That is new."

"The boat will be sold and you shall reap your share immediately. Think how pleased she might be with that offer — and displeased by your rejection."

Hanks said, "I'll decide after the militia parade."

"Parade and barbecue," Johnny said.

"Parade, barbecue and drinks," Offutt said.

As usual, Offutt missed no business opportunity. Without too much effort, he discovered a pie-eyed quartermaster with whom he swapped a jug of whiskey for the large flag they needed to adorn their flagpole.

Offutt gave the flag to Abraham, who raised it smartly. Offutt and Abraham looked up at the colors in silence. Then a huge alligator came up, near the boat, yawning pink, yellow and teeth. Offutt winced and drew back, his hands up in fright. Abraham did not stir.

Abraham said, "Don't they but make noises, Offutt? At night?"

"I don't know. Mostly, at night, I'm sleeping."

"So I hear. You snore," Abraham said.

Offutt made a gator sound, a deep bass frog-like guttural.

"You do hear them," Abraham said.

"Course, I hear them. Gators, frogs," Offutt said, then imitated a bullfrog expertly.

"I wish I could do that," Abraham said.

"You do better, you talk like a politician. More people can do frogs or gators."

"I do want to distinguish myself, link my name up to some cause," Abraham said.

Offutt laughed, a real guffaw.

When he caught his breath, he said, "Lincoln, you are the darndest — didn't I tell you? You sound just like a politician. 'link my name up to some cause.' You are good."

"If I could make the Sangamon navigable, I could be the Dewitt Clinton of Illinois," Abraham said, eyes with stars in them. "I'd gladly throw in with Henry Clay if he'd clear the Sangamon. A step at a time on a long road."

"Well, just remember, there is profits to be had in canals, boy. You need not do all for public good. You can do some private good at the same time and nobody will ever blame you."

Offutt then resumed his imitations of frogs and gators, interspersed with various bird songs that he knew. He could do horses, too, well and recognizably.

CHAPTER THIRTY-TWO

When they came back to the boat, Johnny was all excited. Johnny was angry at Abraham's shrugging response to what he reported. They had seen the noon drill, a big parade at Fort Jefferson, with both militia and Army troops in formation. Abraham had stood out among them in indifference to their maneuvers which, although clumsy from inadequate practice, was conducted with high spirits. A few of the men stumbled and fell from premature inebriation as well. Now, on their return to their boat, as the guard boy departed in the wagon, Johnny lashed out.

"You don't think much of them?" he asked his brother.

"Always be kind to soldiers," Abraham said, echoing their Pa.

The fact is that Abraham was sensitive on the point. He wanted soldiers to do their duty. When they got word years back that redcoats had burned Washington, Ma had told young Abraham and then he'd asked if the Indians were going to get them — the Indians killed his grandpa, after whom he had been named — and Ma soothed him, stroking his brow and saying soldiers were out to protect him, soldiers he could not see. He was never sure. What he saw today depressed him.

"Cheer, that's what you ought to have done. Be patriotic," Johnny said.

"You want to be a soldier now?" Abraham asked, with a grim smile.

"Better than farming," Johnny said.

"And eat hard tack and drink tough coffee?" Abraham asked Johnny, foreseeing trouble in the ranks if Johnny were in uniform.

"And we had more this winter?" Johnny shot back.

"Best you stick close to home," Abraham said back.

Johnny said, "I might conquer Mexico. Ain't we got a right to?"

Abraham shook his head.

Breaking off now from communicating with any of them, Abraham thought about Ann Rutledge at his leisure, and being alone. Her face and blonde curls came easily to his mind's eye, smiling. Had she written a letter to him? Had she sent it at the store or post office of New Salem? Had it gone off in the mail clerk's saddlebag? Had it been sorted at the Springfield post office and given to go by boat to Saint Louis? Was the letter to him in New Orleans here, almost within his reach, in this city? So near and yet so far. Would he get to New Orleans and be disappointed?

That night, without any other recreation, Offutt set a debate in motion to try his strength against Abraham. Offutt said that Jackson hated the bank.

"Clay hates the Bank as much as Jackson did," Abraham said.

Offutt caught the move: Abraham the joke-teller was challenging Offutt. If Offutt was a Clay man but not for Jackson, the equal old hater of banks, Offutt was politically inconsistent.

"That's where the American Plan comes in," Offutt said. "Henry Clay will make us prosperous. Clay'll spend money on roads and canals and bridges."

"And clear streams and rivers?" Abraham asked.

Offutt had never met a man so willing to acknowledge his ignorance and ask even simple, child-level questions as Abraham. Abraham's curiosity was a phenomenon, as constant and inexhaustible as Niagara. No risk of ridicule would stint this man's desire to know. Where had all of his curiosity come from? Offutt was curious about that.

Abraham's curiosity, which had so surprised Offutt earlier, no longer surprised him. Offutt, as whiggish as any entrepreneur, gave a complete and concise answer.

"Clay seeks the best union ever known on earth since man mounted the stage of existence. Navigable waters is part of his plan, knitting the country together. Clay say that's why we put stars on our flag, to give us something to aim at."

"Clay'll clear the Sangamon?" Abraham asked.

"No question, Abe, he'll clear the Sangamon and cut canals all over Illinois. You know the canal out to Louisville, the Portland Locks?" Offutt asked.

"I should. I helped build it," Abraham said.

"Do tell."

"Got my first silver dollars from the canal company. And Johnny."

"Johnny?" Offutt asked. It surprised him, Abraham and his step-brother, on such a trip together.

"Ask him. He and I got thirteen dollars a month, skilled labor."

"What skill?"

"Measuring, marking, helping surveyors, plus poling rafts."

"Not digging."

"Not digging. Slaves did the digging."

"Better than their plantations, I suppose," Offutt said.

"Food and medical, clothes, a roof, four to a shanty," Abraham said.

"Some Irishmen have less," Offutt said. That the slaves' earnings went to their masters neither one said nor needed to say.

"Don't let's get into Irishmen or I'll have to go into my stories," Abraham said.

"Bejabbers, you do just that," Offutt said, clapping his hands now for Irish stories, of which (as he was certain) Abraham had a great store. So the night passed pleasantly prior to sleep.

CHAPTER THIRTY-THREE

Drifting nearer to the shore, better for the larger craft to pass their slow boat, Abraham could hear the *rat-a-tat-tat-tat-tat* of woodpeckers. It was a matter of wonder to him that these birds never rested their heads from banging so enthusiastically into trees. How did their heads never ache, their neck muscles never get sore?

The flatboat proceeded past Alton, where pretty girls giggled and Johnny wanted to stop but Offutt required that *The Ark of the New Covenant* — he dubbed the boat by that name — press on toward Cairo, where they tied up for the night and had a catfish dinner with roast corn and black-eyed peas, which the crew appreciated for long absence of such tasty fare.

At Alton, at a dry goods merchant's, they bought a lead to drop with their rope, to measure depths in the muddy and murky Mississippi.

Once Johnny had done with dropping the lead for the fun of it and pulling it back up out of the river as fast as he could, the lead was tucked to the side of the cabin top. Next to the lead and its rope was a wooden box that held the dry, torn strips of paper used for cleansing. It was Johnny's job to keep that box filled. Hanks and Johnny went down to have something to eat while Offutt lay back atop the cabin to nap, his top hat over his face. Abraham at the bow, pole in hand, was on duty. The flatboat rose and fell very slightly and regularly. The surface was smoother than ever earlier on their journey, banks out of sight. It was as if they were at sea. The craft floated noiselessly and without pause.

Abraham only felt the intake and exhalation of each breath. He was the eye of earth. He stood and saw. He alone was conscious and the clear sky and muddied waters were all he saw or could imagine now, Moses at the burning tree, I am who am, I am I am I am I am, this moment at the bow of the little flatboat he had had a hand in making, Abraham never felt more a disembodied spirit.

Then he felt his legs come back to him, almost falling. He shuffled to maintain his footing on the wooden floor that separated him neatly from the bottom of the catfish-crawling Mississippi. He had seemed briefly but a small child in the sun but now sensed that he was a dweller on the edge of the stage on which humans stood. Between childhood and age, he flowed and breathed and defied time. Unlike his old man, Abraham's grip was not tight and fisted. His light touch he learned from his loom-weaving angel mother and his laughing sister, Sally. They would have loved to have been in the sunshine here on the river.

CHAPTER THIRTY-FOUR

The confluence with the great Ohio, which stretched way back to Kentucky, and was the first big river Abraham had crossed, at age seven, his angel mother then still alive, and poor sister Sally. The gloomy Ohio.

Today, in early spring on a sunny day, the same river sparkled. Warblers, robins, cardinals flew about the fringes of the river, making their ecstatic calls.

"Sounds like somebody's running the machine back there," Offutt said, grinning broadly, showing the gap between his large two front teeth. He said this in a wistful tone, adding, "Abram, you ever wish you had a beak?"

"No, Denny."

"Well, I have seen the courtship of birds and especially of parakeets that you see in Louisiana, you'll see them, too. And there is nothing more obvious than how they do enjoy the kissing and biting of their beaks. They hardly ever let go, and the oooh and ooooh they keep making persuades me that I would be a happier man with a beak."

"If the missus had a beak, too," Abraham said.

That got Offutt to laughing and he repeated, "if the missus had a beak, too," until he bent over, coughing.

A dove landed on their top deck, then another and another until a flock of thirty or more white doves were doing their pigeon-toed walk and turning their head sideways to see if they could make out any better what this craft was, who these men were and where they were heading.

Hungry as he ever was, Abraham was not thinking of killing and eating his new river friends, whose cooing company he enjoyed until Johnston came bolting up out of the hatch and they flew away, startled, as one.

"Should have told me, Abe. I could have snuck up with the shotgun," Johnston said.

"You'd have shot me, if not yourself in the foot," Abraham said.

"What you got to say something like that? You never even seen me shoot. I'd like to see you shoot something."

Abraham let it pass, thinking how much more enjoyable the company of cooing doves were to his step brother's.

CHAPTER THIRTY-FIVE

After kissing the wide Ohio, they spent less than a day each at New Madrid and Memphis. Offutt had the rest wait on the boat while he tended to "business." It was a form of business in which he left with money and returned without money or any apparent purchases, smelling of both alcohol and perfume.

"That's the kind of business I want to run," Johnny said.

En route to Vicksburg, Offutt and Abraham talked. As the current moved them along at a leisurely pace, rowing was needless but eyes were needed on the river for snags or bars.

"Were you from Kentucky, like Hanks?" Offutt asked, lighting up a cigar in great puffs, tossing the loco out into the dark, where it hissed when it kissed the Mississippi.

"I was born in Hardin County," Abraham said.

"Let me guess, to Virginians or Carolinians, I suppose?"

"My father was born in Virginia, my mother, too. She was a bastard," Abraham said.

"You don't say," Offutt said. "So was my mother. Base-borns are known to be more lively, in body and mind. It's a fact can be proved and it's also in Shakespeare. You ever read, Abe?"

"I read often."

"Well, do not neglect Shakespeare. Or Bobby Burns, neither."

Abraham went on about his life.

"We moved to Indiana, Spencer County, in 1816."

Offutt made a wolf howl.

"I been through Spencer County, wolf country, thick as thieves, wolves there. I trotted through fast as I could. Didn't see you, boy."

"Most people wouldn't. We built our cabin deep in the tall trees. So dense it was dark night and day. We took a lamp to see if the sun rose until we cleared the ground around."

"No, Abe, that wasn't your dense forest. That dark was the year itself, 1816, the year with no summer. I sold land in Indiana to a lot of farmers in Virginia, frozen, barren, dark Virginia that year."

"I remember it as dark. Is that why? I thought it was the trees."

"No. Not trees, young man. Worst year ever in this country, in the wide world even. In the Tower of London, the King's chamber pot froze solid. God's truth, Switzerland was snowed under in mid-July. They had frost on the Italian

111

prairie, no spaghetti grew to ripe and some starved. So, in Richmond, Virginia, what was true elsewhere brought me a lot of interested buyers. Lots I couldn't give away the year before stood for a pretty penny in 1816, Abraham. That's when I learned the secret, that timing is everything. Timing. Is. Everything. When it is time, no force on earth can stop whatever is due, and when it is not time, you are just banging your head into a stone wall and the stone wall will keep winning. Until it's time. That's all I can tell you, wisdom of forty years speaking."

"How do you know when it's time?" Abraham asked.

"The same old way, 'by their fruits shall ye know.' Until then, you just keep your powder dry and cast your bread upon the waters," Offutt said.

After Vicksburg came Natchez, and smaller spots nearly identical to one another, one long string of settlements all the way to Baton Rouge and, finally, New Orleans.

At the third range of the Chickasaw bluffs the weather was cold and disagreeable. A strong wind blew, the first one so constant and strong that Abraham thought of the howling wind of the terrible winter. Now, however, in milder temperatures, without snow and only a drizzly rain, he in his woolen jacket was modestly comfortable. Shielded also by the overhanging deck and high walls, he was not snug but neither did he suffer as he had in the Lincolns' tiny, stinking cabin. Above Abraham, playing and disappearing and reappearing in the clouds, was one hawk, slate-colored, circling, no doubt alert for the chance that a fish or some critter on the banks or in the trees would expose themselves carelessly, whereupon that hawk would drop like a stone and hit the target with open claws. Just now, high overhead, circling lazily, the same bird seemed an imperturbable and stoic sentry between worlds. Abraham knew that hawks, of all birds, would be his most constant company. From Indiana to New Orleans he had seen countless hawks the first trip, red-tailed, prairie, marsh, great-footed, winter, black hawks. No mile of the first journey, nor of the second, did not include hawk sightings. *It must be hell on the little critters with so many hawks about*, Abraham thought.

Offutt directed them to a landing with a path that, he said, led to an old army fort. He intended a break from being on the dull and monotonous river on a bad day.

"Look for treasure, boys," he said. "Bring a pail and pick and shovel."

They did so, leaving Johnston to guard the boat and the trio of Offutt, Hanks and Abraham following the narrow, twisting path, running into green briars but proceeding through despite scratches, until they came to the top of a hill. As promised, the stone and rotten wood ruins of an army post persisted to exhibit a kind of footprint that Uncle Sam had once been up here, overlooking the river. Offutt pointed out a couple of places to dig. Nobody thought they would find anything, nor did they believe Offutt thought they would either. It was a lark for an hour. They found worms and a broken, rusted canteen.

They left after taking a good, long look at the river, here today a long, broad grey-brownish ribbon cutting through mostly forest and uncleared land. Several flatboats were en route, a steamboat was chugging north, doubtless to Saint Louis. Acoustics were good enough to hear shouting at a distance as evidence of humanity's concerns with their own concerns no matter who stood upon the banks in the old fort's site looking down after having failed to discover treasure.

CHAPTER THIRTY-SIX

Under plank sail and Old Glory, they were now fast coming into Mississippi as they drifted below Memphis. All aboard the *Ark* were above deck, Hanks and Offutt at the bow, Abraham at their tiller along with Johnny in the stern. Had the flatboat been better designed, the rear wall of the craft would have been several boards higher, above waist, chest-high. As it was, short-blocked, it would be easy to fall off, especially a man as tall as Abraham.

Up in back of the boat came a sound, distant at first, a whirring, a faint fluttering, some sort of stifled cries or coos, what seemed to be an unseen but bustling tumult. The sky darkened into a weird dimness for the late morning. Then, all at once, it became clear and manifest as if out of nowhere: above them flowed a huge stream of birds, carrier pigeons headed southward to the Gulf of Mexico from some parts north.

Abraham had seen such flocks but never had circumstances or reason to attend to the passage of so many animals. Over the canopy of the Indiana woods he had occasionally heard or seen some of these migrating birds, not in Illinois but he had only been a year in Illinois. Maybe they did not fly over Macon County. In any case, the enormity of this stampede of the sky was its startling fact. What had been dimming became a dark shadow that blotted out the sun.

Abraham smelled a kind of powdery, acrid scent. Bird smell, flock smell. As they flew over, their wings in unison made a kind of noise like a muted fire, snapping of twigs. The little flatboat — for little it now seemed — was as much in the dark as if the sun had set. He thought of the Bible's reference to God's voice coming out of the whirlwind in the Book of Job. Then the flock was gone and it was light again. They continued drifting through Creation south to New Orleans.

The most feared thing on the trip downriver was in the river itself — the underwater snag. A snag could be small or large, sharp or stubby. While a stubby, rotted, small one would be known by a hit and a bump, at worst a jolt and a jerk, a sudden stop and release, a sharp and large sawyer could bring down a steamboat, let alone a craft as frail as four-man hog barge. With all hands swimming or just sinking in fast current without sight or sound of man or land, a snag could dispose of men, cutting them up and leaving them for the gators and catfish. They would be "late" and then, finally, "feared lost" until "presumed dead" as hope faded among family and friends and their very memories proved as mortal as themselves. The list of those lost on the river was a very long list, itself lost to human view.

Abraham recalled one particular snag upon which he and Gentry had perched. By luck, Abraham calling for Gentry to leap to one side following him, Gentry did with blind faith. To their mutual relief, their boat lurched precariously but then slid back into the river. It was an experience Abraham did not care to renew.

He realized upon the river more than anywhere else how indifferent nature was to human desires. Even the warm, lush-seeming, slow, bucolic, facially-beautiful nature between Louisiana on one far bank and Mississippi on the other was indifferent to his and Gentry's living or dying. Life went on. The Father of Waters rolled on. They had survived. But life would go on if they had not, the same turtle just swimming by would swim by. Back that day, their little leaky boat had resumed its slow, balky passage under the noonday sun of the lower delta. Except that Abraham knew, and knew on this voyage with Offutt: the waters of the river and its creatures will always roll on, run on, swim on, fly on no matter whether they arrived, all alive, in New Orleans on this flatboat.

CHAPTER THIRTY-SEVEN

On this bright, sunny morning, the surface of the broad river was alive and sparkling with a shine that made you squint and hold your hand up over your eyes. They were in about the middle of a moving armada. Ahead of them, as far as could be seen for miles on this unusual straight stretch, as well as behind them, back as far as the bend some two miles back, were flatboats, barges, small craft and a couple of steamboats, one headed south, the other tooting its whistle, its crew's loud and shouted curses carrying far, heading north through thick traffic. Oblivious to this stream of American commerce, this flex of muscle by the American economy, a heavy-lidded Mississippi kite was busy with sudden pokes of its neck catching small lizards off the bark of a dead cypress floating toward the Arkansas side of the river. Neither the commerce nor the kite stopped but both proceeded about their business.

They floated past the decrepit building of a worn-out Indian trader, his porch near collapse, the sign askew identifying the agent. Offutt was much tempted to stop.

"What say we stop and trade, Hanks?"

"Ask your captain."

"I'm asking you. You got a tongue."

"I suppose I do."

"Well, you're being paid. Tell me what you think."

"I'm paid to row and to watch and to work, not to think and to talk."

"Don't be like that. I'm sorry if I hurt your feelings. Shall we stop?"

"If you say so. But I can't see you getting the best of an Indian trader."

"Watch me. Stop."

It was as if Hanks had dared Offutt in a game.

They stopped at this humble store, from which a ramshackle pier stretched one long, skinny, beggarly arm for anything that might drift by.

"Why are we stopping?" Abraham asked, coming up.

"Offutt's going to trade."

"It looks like a storm," Abraham said, inviting attention to an increasing wind and cold that they had not noticed.

"All right, move on."

It was stormy and the better part of discretion was to find a sturdier pier. By great good fortune, they soon found a landing and a nearby plantation at which they made trade for fresh goods. It was a cotton-and-corn plantation

117

mostly but, like many, it supported orchards and fields for subsistence crops and to trade. The best bargain Offutt made was for a bushel of sweet potatoes, just dug, for the price of a mere fifty cents. Offutt knew he could get three to four dollars for the bushel in New Orleans but he was far more inclined to feed himself and the crew on these spuds. Bacon and hardtack lost its savor after a time. The current was stronger here, the days seemed shorter, certainly their excitement was higher as they thought of the city becoming near and real instead of a distant and abstract goal. This excitement, together with their constant companion, hunger, allowed these sweet potatoes, roasted, to top their corn-meal-fried-catfish and that partridge pie as the most delicious of their flatboat meals.

"You didn't get the best of the Indian trader," Hanks said.

"We didn't stop."

"You didn't get the best of him any way you want to say it."

"Why, you were right, Hanks."

"It was a good idea not to stop."

"You know, Hanks, I am making you Alternate Captain. Whenever Abraham is not on deck, you are the Captain."

Hanks smiled and nodded.

"For another ten cents a day on full days."

"Ain't going to be no full days."

"I know. That's why I asked."

Offutt thought.

"All right then, Hanks, Captain on a full day and you get ten cents more."

They shook hands.

Abraham had watched the transaction in silence, pressing his hand up to his mouth not to laugh.

"Abraham, shake hands with Alternate Captain Hanks here."

The cousins shook hands, for the first time in their lives. They had hugged, they had stood and talked, but they had never, until now, simply shaken hands.

They ate well that night, joking freely and telling stories, Offutt sang a hymn in good humor, the others found a couple of bawdy tunes worth raising voice to, and their room at the stern seemed warmer even then the places they had left. They had formed something of a home on the water.

CHAPTER THIRTY-EIGHT

The next morning broke along with cries of mirthful-seeming birds. Nature seemed to celebrate their harmony. Birdsong was all around them, from cardinals, town buntings, meadow larks, a chorus of sparrows, the plover and the strutting, piping kingfisher, all in motion, all cheering the rising sun. One would not think of this low swampish spot as sickly, a miasmatic place of fevers and pinworms — as it surely was — on this fine but muggy morning. Insect-rich, especially with flying insects like mosquitoes, it supported all of these birds, lizards and other animals. But clouds of flying, biting insects suggested to them that they cast off and head for mid-stream, underway again for New Orleans. They noted that the churning waters of the White River were red, and wondered if the Red River's waters would be clear. Arkansas was losing its red clay and Louisiana was obviously gaining some red silt downstream.

That night there was no help for it, they had to anchor at a bar. With the wind, they kept knocking into and off the bar, bumping all night. Nobody slept very long or very well that night.

On the bar, curious animals appeared, sometimes only one and shyly, obscured by a cottonwood tree or droop of Spanish moss, sometimes two or three gathered together, sometimes in concert, moving or at rest, in a group. A woodchuck, a beaver, a muskrat. The sound of a woodpecker, several wood-peckers. Offutt had pointed out an ivory bill, quite a large woodpecker. The noisiest bunches came along in the cypress stands or broad sycamores here and there, lively, comical green parrots with yellow heads and red masks about their eyes. Their sounds were a cacophony of pie social uproars. Mockingbirds, larks, swallowtails darting and diving after flies, green and blue and yellow king-fishers, herons. Owls hooted every so often. White birds — ibises? cranes? — walked on stilts over mudflats, ducks sprawled all along certain banks, quacking and grousing about life. Abraham heard enough cuckoos in April to last him a lifetime. The shrieks of some other birds seemed exotic to his ears. Hawks and broad-winged eagles reigned over the cacophony of warblers, whistlers, flying, gliding over a million insects that made cicada buzzes or cricket chirps, over the galumph of bullfrogs, how much bigger they must grow down here to make noises like that. Abraham had seen hawks and falcons before but never an albino falcon, which startled him as if it were the ghost of one. A loudly-buzzing hive of bees passed terrifyingly close over his head looking for a stump across the river apparently. He'd laughed at himself for jumping when their noise was the

119

most frightening part of the event. They came close enough to heard, and to terrify him, but not so close he ought to have jumped. He was never alone up above decks now. Nature, rich, abundant, overflowing nature never left him be as the flatboat drifted southward.

CHAPTER THIRTY-NINE

The journey gradually exhausted everyone's stories and jokes, talking after a week together was fraught with sore points. Men who started downriver as the best of friends sometimes grew into deadly enemies before reaching New Orleans. Sometimes bodies were discovered. Identities typically unknown, features even unrecognizable as human, faces eaten, they were supposed men who fell or jumped to end regretted lives. Always suspected, however, was that their lives were cut short for snoring too loud or for emptying the whiskey jug.

Had it not been for weather and the storms, passage through hazards, many hazards missed and passed invisibly, would have been intolerably long, dull and tedious for all. As it was, the travelers with Offutt thought most about food, second about being warm and dry, third about food again. Some days, caught mid-stream when a curtain of fog descended, often with rain, they would have to anchor in flat despair. Under a leaking roof, breathing the smoke of a damp fire, both did nothing to take away the chill of a bleak and dark day stuck in place.

Human nature being what it is, necessity proved mother of invention to pass the time a bit faster. Music worked best. Abraham had brought his jew's harp, Johnny handled a barrel as a sort of drum, Hanks had a flute and Offutt a three-string fiddle. It was strange how much better these all sounded on the river, so much that they heard cheers and applause from boats nearby, men who had never crossed the road to hear music in their lives ashore.

Offutt and Abraham read, though neither Hanks nor Johnny did. The latter two moved about the boat performing the needed work of slopping the hogs, removing the dead — Goodby's wild pigs had seemed healthy but may have brought something catchy aboard that took down six hogs — acting the role of butcher, mucking, and doing trifling tasks, shoring up a timber, inspecting and adjusting cargo, trying to fix the clay-and-brick stove and chimney arrangement (which never actually resulted in less smoke or more heat). Offutt and Abraham, in rotation, manned the boat's bow or stern sweeps and, at rest, read anything they each had brought, sharing their texts and on occasion discussing them.

More than playing music or reading or tasks, great or small, the ongoing scenery of nature at large was inexhaustibly interesting. Unlike the familiar fields and woods within sight of cabin-dwellers, or the panorama that they passed on horseback or as oxen footed forward joltingly and slowly, the scenes of wildlife and plant-life along, on and over the river sped by fast and kept changing. The banks were lower or higher, raising up into towering bluffs at times, 150 to 200 feet high. For a two-mile stretch the second Chickasaw bluff, all clay and varicolored, dribbled like a great melting candle, red, yellow, black and deep lead. As Nature melted the land into the river, it bled in such colors. Thousands of holes, the nests of bank swallows, were busy and occupied despite their seeming jeopardy in the constant avalanches. Gulls, bald-headed eagles — several fighting and biting, snatching pieces of a deer carcass at the juncture of land and river — they passed, as they were in turn passed by a large flock of goldfinches, and by small mobs of blue jays, cardinals and big, flapping cranes. Beyond the Devil's Raceground, which proved at least in high water to be a tamer affair than its name implied, its rapids and rocks a few feet below them, the stream was often alive with fish, leaping frogs and alligators at times, birds flew over singly and in flocks and by the thousands at times, silently and high, specks, other times so low that they seemed touchable by reaching up. They saw geese, many cardinals, flashes of red as they darted and claimed higher branches in the sun, some greenish Carolina wrens, purple finches punctuating the land-scape as well. When rain abated, they walked a large bar or island. John Hanks with a single shot brought down a large blue crane, which made for a salty, gamey, tough meal.

Another attempt to shake the blues or cure boredom — challenges to race to a stated point — were dangerous. It was a sheer gamble for nothing as two crafts, flatboats or any other, competed. The degree of torment then self-imposed to win and not to lose made for accidents and collisions, sometimes with dire results. It was rare for a race to end peaceably or without rancor, the argument between newly-met strangers of who actually won a race, crossed a point first, was a terrible and serious thing, given armed men.

Offutt had instructed them not to give or ever accept a challenge. Although their flatboat, rigged and heavily-loaded as it was, would surely lose any contest by a clear margin, there was no advantage to be had in trying to compete. The least that would happen is an angry and derisive taunt that they had not tried to win. Abraham was typically the one who was able to speak good-naturedly and decline challenges graciously, with a joke.

"Best not today," Abraham would say, for example. "I've got the trots today, we would have raced you yesterday, though."

The third Chickasaw bluffs were probably equally splendid monuments to the creative and exultant joy of a Creator God, but He had brought a cold and disagreeable fog to come down, along with a strong wind blowing that led them to hunch up and hold their heads down, turtle-like, passing the sights without looking. They ran to the right of a long island, upon which Indians had pitched teepees and had fires going. A bear skin covered one of the teepees. The Indians — Osage, Offutt suggested — looked to be warmer than they were, and better fed. But there was no stopping.

Two flocks of American teals flew south over them. Chattering, chittering cacophonous parakeets were now numerous in the woods of the banks. A large flock of Sand Hill cranes proved the most dignified, amazing sight. How at first they glided, then powerfully stroked their wings to elevate up, up into the air, up toward the clouds. They were headed south, as well as a flock of spring tail ducks and another of hurrying cedar birds that seemed to be following the cranes' lead. They saw a swan on a bar ahead and not far off that Johnston shot at without success. It was funny to see the swan take no precaution, standing still and staring at Johnston before, during and after the shot. Abraham touched the end of his rifle and said, "One's enough, don't waste your powder."

Each night they landed their presence generated an uproar among the plentiful swamp sparrows, both those in the high grass and on the mud itself. Sometimes they were anchored among fifteen or twenty other flatboats, other nights by themselves. No matter by what standard they might judge — except being the most recently-constructed — their humble flatboat was always smaller, more obviously home-built, oddly-designed and even smokier and smellier than any craft near them. Given the hogs, they were offered "Pee-yew" and nose-holding salutes by some of the rougher rivermen. Such insults they bore with a grin, sometimes saying, "We lived with the pigs so long, we can't smell them anymore."

CHAPTER FORTY

One morning, early, they heard a noise of a violent storm coming that turned out to be the largest flock of merganzers any of them ever saw. They were heard before they were seen, they were not long overhead and then they were gone. Nature did her tricks and vanished like a magician, leaving an audience in awe wondering how it was done. How had so many birds come to be hatched, to live, to find food, to flock together, to head south at the same time and keep up?

Astonishing swarms of grackles sometimes landed on trees ashore. With grackles it was not so much their noise — although they were noisy — as their smell. These were birds that never bathed, it seemed. Their stink was pronounced.

Hundreds of gulls might play over a bar, diving and gliding, rising and falling, making their cock-of-the-air cries and indignant screeches as one stole a fish from the other one's beak. Fat geese, but not the spindly, boney gulls, made good meals and nobody was tempted to offer the gulls buckshot, although they might have hit a half-dozen or a dozen with a single discharge.

Hanks and Johnny fished with strong and resilient willow wood poles off the bow, meeting with success often enough but occasionally losing lines and even poles to curious alligators or lurking river-bottom catfish.

Shortly after a drenching shower ended, the most wonderful rainbow, deeply colored and huge, arched over them and the river, "hung by God like a good omen," Offutt cried. Nobody else had words for it though they all felt something about the radiant and glowing, magical image above that seemed to be around and to embrace them. Abraham, a great and close Bible reader, could not help but think of Noah looking up to see the sign of a covenant not to destroy the Earth again as He had.

They caught a giant catfish, at least thirty pounds — bigger, it would have carried away the line and pole — that Johnny stabbed once but would not go near again. It took a long hour dying, and Abraham suffered every minute waiting for the gasps to stop. Then Hanks got to work with instructions.

"The skin is very tough," Hanks told Johnston. "It's almost like leather. Strike and tear down the skin, making strips, narrow strips, and I'll pull those pieces down with my pliers."

Johnny made his rows of long slices, after which Hanks got a grip of the top of a strip and pulled, taking down that tough skin strip by strip until the fish could be cut up for greasy, smelly pieces to cook. Offutt suggested salt, pepper

and corn meal, and to use up the last of their butter, which, when done, actually made the catfish palatable, if not delicious. It was their best meal next after a
partridge pie, which had included yams, honey and special sauce inside the but-
tered flour crust. Usually their meals were on the fly, a cut of bacon from what
was hanging by the chimney, some cracker, cheese or hardtack.

"Rainbow catfish," Offutt said. "Dropped down from heaven onto our
plates."

CHAPTER FORTY-ONE

A glittering of hummingbirds, iridescent, sparkling sun-catchers, flew about in zig-zag glory. Within the bouquet, some flew, some hovered, some flew backwards. Giddily tossing themselves up at the old sky, the shimmer unfurled a new canopy. The tunes sewed gossamer, stitching miles of nothingness, turning at a touch all colors the blue and cloudless. Alight with them, the sky hummed with hummingbirds, once empty, suddenly a rich space of unimagined birdliness.

It was like nothing Abraham had ever seen or imagined.

It seemed like nobody had ever spied music on the wing before Abraham this day or surely he would have read of it. No traveler could see these miracles of the air without shouting that news from the rooftops. It was incredible to be alive on the same planet at the same time as these God-made glories.

Then, miracle of miracles, one came to him, one in particular, one that seemed to have bug eyes and to be staring back at him as Abraham this banal day guided the flatboat downriver. Their mutual stare lasted no more than a minute but after this one had flown off and away, Abraham thought long about the tune. Their iridescence faded in memory as his mind rooted in their mysteries.

Didn't they think? What did they think? What was going on in their minds? In his own face, what did his hummingbird see?

Surely, the Indians once considered such a sighting ominous. These days, such episodes were wasted. Nobody aboard would care, not one person Abraham knew would hear him with interest or excitement.

Soon after, Johnny shouted for everybody to come see several dark brown turkey buzzards, some still swooping down, like four-pound hens with two-yard wingspans. The crowd of six to eight of them were biting at a half-rotted deer carcass by the bank, hissing as they fought one another with what must have been razor-sharp beaks. Their long necks darting made Abraham think of snakes, and he just hated snakes. They were not creatures he wanted to watch, unblinking snakes or buzzards, especially eating a carcass. He left the rest to enjoy that particular entertainment.

As a spatter of rain from a bank of black clouds, along with flashes of lightning and the rumble of thunder heralded what was to come, two more flatboats tied up. The crews of neither of these boats stayed strangers long to one another, nor to the small ugly duckling that was the Offutt Empire's fleet. All shouted greetings, one boat being from St. Louis, hauling lumber — Abraham renewed his thoughts about chopping wood in St. Louis — and the other from Tennessee, with a mixed cargo, mostly sixty hogs.

"You can tell," Johnny said, telling Abraham with a gesture to his nose. "Glad I only got our pens to clean."

The rain started in earnest now, coming down between the original splatters and an imminent drenching. The two brothers stood over the scuttle-hole to climb down, neither one presuming to go first.

Abraham allowed Johnny to scramble down the ladder. They both were already soaked.

They assembled in the stern cabin. The scent of the farm was not faint. Pig was redolent in the air.

Johnny paid Hanks fifteen cents for a quarter-plug to smoke, along with use of Hanks's pipe, after Hanks was done. Johnny got pale after five great inhaled puffs and had to leave the cabin to retch up above.

"He don't know about letting it out," Hanks said, his eyes twinkling, almost tears from the humor of seeing it.

"Misspent youth," Abraham said. "Ha, he was *eating* it."

They both laughed but broke off as Johnny returned, then passed the pipe back to Hanks without saying more.

"Storms' most over," Johnny said, as if he had only left to check on the weather.

"Stopped raining?" Abraham asked.

"Offutt's on the St. Louis boat," Johnny said, ignoring Abraham's question. "Playing cards and drinking. I hear him singing."

Hanks said, "He do like to sing and the rest. Let's hope he don't bet the boat on a card."

"Can he do that?" Johnny asked, in sudden and obvious anxiety.

Hanks said, "Man's property, he can do what he wants with what's his own. That's the law, with few exceptions."

"Mechanic's lien. We got rights," Abraham said.

"I taught you that," Hanks said.

"You got your farm. I've just got a piece of this boat. I got to remember," Abraham said.

Johnny shook his head. The "mechanic's lien" was over his head. All he could imagine now was Offutt betting the boat on the turn of a card.

Johnny said, "Don't seem right, not right at all."

"You don't like it, change the law," Abraham said.

"What? Run for legislature?" Johnny asked.

"Legislator. Yes, run for legislator. Legislators are men like anybody else.

Remember, Posey was a legislator, and you've met others. Judge Porter back in Indiana."

"I got other things to do with my life than change laws," Johnny said.

Hanks smiled as he sewed a torn sock, saying, "So do I, I got smoking to do and this here sock."

Their laugh together was a brief renewal of the spirit of the evening before as the storm passed with one last roll of a grumbling rumble.

CHAPTER FORTY-TWO

Nights followed days on the river. Maintaining vigilance by tossing lead was nerve-wracking even with torches burning and poling.

"Toss them," Abraham would call out to Johnny.

"Toss them yourself," Johnny would sass back, not wanting to handle their slimy leads and drag them back up from the mud in the river. Each had to toss the weights out over the water and feel the bump when they hit bottom, then take up slack and measure. It was a tedious chore that needed to be done. Even if they were in mid-channel, and they were rarely in mid-channel. No flatboat could be in mid-channel with traffic. Their slow boat, lower in the water than most craft on these waters — canoes were lower but faster — had to edge its way down the river, tossing the lead to gauge the depth.

"Now," Abraham said. "Or I give you what-for."

"Give me what-for? You ain't my Pa."

"I am your older brother, *in loco parentis*."

"In Pocohontas? You talking Indian talk now?"

"It's law. It means that, absent Pa, I am your master. Now, you do it or I give you what-for."

Johnny cussed and tossed the lead with a splash intended to hit Abraham but which fell short.

"Eighteen feet," Johnny said, knowing Abraham would ask for another measure to see if the bottom was rising or falling or the same.

"Again," Abraham said.

"I ain't no slave," Johnny said. "I'm a man."

"Not yet."

Johnny was angry, younger than Abraham and not yet twenty-one. But he would be soon and then, why, then he'd rebel. He'd be a man and could do what he wanted or show his fists to his brother.

"Six," was the next reading, danger, barely fair warning of a bar or of a snag.

"Six?" Abraham asked in a quick bark.

"Teen. Sixteen," Johnny said, grinning at his joke.

Abraham sighed.

Nobody aboard but Hanks and Abraham, least of all Johnny, and certainly not Offutt, had any faint idea or experience or recollection of hazards on the river, of dangerous bends, sudden rapids, a whole immediate series of obstacles, and how long they might last until reaching deep water and a smooth current. Add to that constant traffic, drunken or reckless boatmen in often larger barge-like boats, steamboats, fog and storms. Unlike Hanks, who had a sort of sixth sense about approaching hazards, Abraham never could tell whether they were heading into trouble or away from it. Hanks and Abraham tried to rotate on duty, never to have Offutt and Johnny the only ones awake except when they were anchored or at a pier. Johnny and Offutt took turns at the bow with the confidence or blithe manner that they each walked on land, ignorant of all dangers until Hanks or Abraham pointed out something to them, calmly as a teacher of spelling.

CHAPTER FORTY-THREE

The admiration between Hanks and Abraham was mutual, lifelong and rarely grudging. From New Salem on, an event stood in the way. By the fluke of Abraham having saved the boat and cargo from immediate and certain disaster by an innovation beyond Hanks's imagination, Offutt had named Abraham captain. Hanks had been hurt by this enough to threaten to leave the boat once it reached St. Louis and "walk home." It made Abraham ponder leadership.

During his trip on the little flatboat with Allen Gentry, there had been no question: Abraham had been in charge. Older, stronger, more experienced on water, generally handier, Abraham literally towered over young Gentry, poor, nervous rich man's son more along for the ride than a hand or crew. It was Abraham who sensed hidden, invisible dangers in the most innocent-seeming bit of bubbles or supposedly harmless floating leafy branch, actually the tip of a hundred-year-old cypress with a fatal hand reaching up to them.

On that trip with Gentry Abraham got no sleep. On ear was ever listening and he was startling awake the entire trip at the sound of a scrape under the hull, the noise of a touch or a tap. A gator beside them, or a turtle bumping, would make a noise, a touch, a tap. Abraham never got a good night's sleep. With Gentry on watch, those slaves had sneaked up and nearly aboard. Had they not, stupidly but luckily, shouted as they charged, swinging clubs, the brawl might have ended them. Abraham considered how they might have been tossed into the river to sink and be eaten by catfish or alligators. And the folks back home would never have a clue as to the fate of their young men. Old Man Gentry would have hired detectives and they would have looked for Abraham incidentally but nothing would ever uncover the crime. Their murderers would yet walk the earth, just as their would-be murderers did walk under the same sun yet.

For sleeping, this trip was generally far better. Abraham was hopeful, just as on that first trip he had felt gnawing and deep despair, of reaching and docking at New Orleans. This second trip, with able-handed John Hanks more than anything, enabled him to sleep. Johnny was helping more each day, grumble though he did, standing atop the cabinhouse with his telescope or seated or lying down taking a nap in the bright sun like some satisfied gator. Their remarkable companion and inimitable employer, Denton Offutt, set the example of simply setting. No man could appear more satisfied, happier than Offutt singing his old Baptist hymns at the top of his voice just as the spirit moved him. Abraham was in awe of the man's capacity for joy.

Offutt was singing and broke off singing mid-song when they approached a "dead boat," one of those mystery craft in which not a soul remained, a flatboat adrift and abandoned. Had its crew-members fought and fallen overboard, then drowned. Had there been a plague? After shouting a few halloes, one left such craft be as bad luck to touch.

Abraham remained hopeful of reaching New Orleans alive.

CHAPTER FORTY-FOUR

Abraham and Allen had stopped over to a small tavern in a village on the Arkansas bank.

"At the tavern there sat a simpleton-looking old fellow, he had long hair and a beard, he looked like a prophet of the Bible whose head knew no razor. His eyes blazed but nobody spoke to him and he spoke to nobody," Abraham said.

"What's he got to do with gators?"

"I'm about to say, stay your patience. We asked, Allen or me, who he was and his name was Lambert, they said. He came down from Kentucky on a flatboat with wife and child, an infant, his son. One morning the baby soiled himself and the wife had him dangling over the side, you know, dipping him up and down to bathe him. All of a sudden up leaped out of the river a gator, mouth open and, of course, grabbed ahold of the boy and disappeared back down into the depths, leaving the wife screaming and the husband with nothing he could do, holding his oar over the river."

"They can stay down forever," Johnny said. "Gators don't have to come up for air."

"They do," Abraham said, "but not right away. And surely the child died quickly. But the wife went crazy and that night jumped overboard and drowned herself. That left only Lambert. He went ashore right there, at the next village, the one we stopped at on the Arkansas shore, and sold all he had for a rifle, balls and powder. He then commenced his campaign, to kill ever gator he could for the rest of his life."

"He'd been doing it long when you saw him?"

"Ten years, they said, at least. They never thought he'd keep it up. But he did hunting and fishing, too, to keep himself alive, sold some of his kills to the tavern, bartered. He had a shanty somewhere, maybe two, folks said. But his whole life was devoted to killing gators."

"Sad story," Johnny said.

"A warning I took to heart," Abraham said. "You won't catch me dangling over the side or swimming in the river. Not here."

"Gators," Johnny said.

"Gators," Abraham said.

Later that same day, they all thought that they had seen the largest flocks possible when they saw what had to be formations of millions of Irish geese or cormorants, darkening the sky more effectively than an eclipse or any number of dark clouds. It was like the end of the world, a prodigious sign of last times, when these birds flew over and in indifferent but orderly progress, line after line, row after row, layers upon layers, passed. One thought of a legion of angels, an army in the sky, an innumerable host. Again, one lacked words. It left them with their mouths open. This was the sight before they came to the Natchez bluffs.

Offutt pointed out the tiny shacks along the shore, unoccupied but tidy-seeming, kept-up. Each had a mill-wheel beside, not turning now.

"Lumber mills," Offutt explained. "In spring, when the river floods for a time into the swamps, the creeks beside each of these mills fills with current and, short though the time be, the owners of these mills come and operate, taking timber in and sawing lumber planks for the summer. All done in great haste. The rest of the time, the mills vacant."

The situation reminded them that the river was not stable but an up and down body of water, with flood and ebb, and was not any longer at its highest or quickest. The fleet had caught the crest to New Orleans and left their flatboat far behind.

"No harm," Offutt said. "They glut the market and get the meanest prices. We will have the best of the bargaining coming along a little later. New Orleans is a great mouth that constantly needs what we are carrying. The only question is price and the matter of price is set by time, time of arrival. A day can make a difference, even an hour. We will be along in a good time and get much better prices than our much faster competitors."

CHAPTER FORTY-FIVE

Nights, tying up at a plantation pier, their torches burning at both sides and at both ends of the flatboat, they all cupped their hands to their mouths and yelled to attract attention, Johnny enjoying this most of all of them.

"Hootee, hootee, gals, your Johnny's heeeere. Come on outta your houses, yeeer Johnny's heeeerooh. Come see your podgeee."

"Not 'podgee,' Johnny, pro-di-gy," Offutt corrected him. Offutt had said that Johnny was a prodigy for knowing how to tie a square knot.

"Come on out and see yeeeer prodeeegeeeee, Johnny Johnston," Johnny shouted.

Abraham's lip curved, but it was not as a smile of pleasure. He thought Johnny was a poor student of the river school. Abraham had learned many more words from Allen Gentry, words Allen got from professors in college. It was not yet within his power to speak as well as some, Abraham thought, but he spoke a whole lot better than his Pa ever would. For himself, here, Abraham had only shouted, "Goods, goods, cheap, cheap, for cash or trade, cash or trade."

Usually, given enough noise, out would come someone with a lantern or a slave or two would arrive with baskets, trading with boats that stopped being a regular but unscheduled occurrence. None yet had brought or offered money, although Offutt did offer cheaply-priced goods for specie.

CHAPTER FORTY-SIX

One twilight as they floated through a slothful and languid segment that was also a part of this great and often wide river, Abraham saw something. It was a shadow, an eddy, a swirl. Something anomalous caught his attention not an instant before the flatboat would be hitting it on the starboard side.

"Snag right!" Abraham called out loudly, the way they made one another alert to hazards.

Many snags, delightfully, turned out to be nothing. The best, most blessed type of relief followed such a false alarm. No one faulted false prophets of disaster on the river. It was only a matter of seconds before one relaxed — or felt the boat crash.

"All clear!" the helmsman could call. Abraham did call out so, words that were mere confirmation of the feeling that all aboard had already had: seconds had passed. They were not going to hit anything, they were not going to drown. At least, not yet.

Another danger was close encounter with large-wake riverboats. These craft, steaming up or going down the great river in the best channels, left the boatmen, all of them, occasional and ribald, taunting competitors on fringes. To the world, the boatmen seemed a peevish, unreliable, tricky lot. With one another, the professionals were a band of brothers and peers, many of them destined (if not doomed) to association with flatboats and the river for the rest of their lives. The one-trip or one-season boatman was not admitted into the fraternity immediately. From such "civilians" purporting to be boatmen the regular boatmen stood apart, usually indifferent and sometimes hostile. As to the riverboats, for old time's sake and past slights, boatmen would not hesitate to deal dirty.

Being thus less than step brothers, those aboard the *Ark* were never comfortable, at rest or in current, to hear even distant voices.

A possible nearby riverboat was dangerous and, in thick fog, invisible. No riverboat steered to avoid collision with a mere flatboat. On the face of it, the rule was intended to provide a right of way understood by both parties. It was the duty of the boatmen to get out of the way. The smaller craft had the assumed better means to take evasive action, being smaller, more flexible, able to run itself into much shallower waters without harm. But the riverboats were faster and, of course, powered by engines that got them up to twenty or thirty miles an hour. As a result, the smaller craft were floating in a universe while, past them, at five times their speed, huge vessels poured by, their high wake jostling and tossing them out of their bunks and making the hogs squeal in panic. From this situation there was no retreat or redress.

Offutt sang a hymn about the perils of life, and the saving grace of the Lord, but never during occasions of bell-ringing, chugging, loud-voiced river-boat passings — one with a lively fiddle playing, apparently from the promenade, perhaps where passengers were dancing — only afterward. During such times all hands braced for an issue and were relieved no end when the steamboat passed, much like the smiting Hand of God. Nobody wrote or spoke of these instances of fear, cold sweat terror. No civilian could understand and no boatmen cared to hear. Stories of actual collisions were not in circulation. They were never told because the most of those involved from the flatboats hit were gone and survivors, whether continuing to pursue their profession and unwilling to bear the stigma of jinx, or simply surviving and being unwilling to look back, were silent but for occasional gloom and mumbled curses when they saw a steamboat coming.

Offutt gently poked Abraham in the ribs with an elbow, nodding for him to notice something on their right. It was a large raft of logs manned and awkwardly directed, spinning a bit as its logs jostled and bobbed.

"Congress land wood," Offutt said quietly.

The rough timbers tied loosely together floated by the flatboat, itself composed mainly of Congress land wood. Somewhere in the woods unseen a screech owl made its eerie whinny.

"Where's all that wood going?" Abraham asked, equally quietly. Sounds traveled far on the Mississippi. Sometimes they could hear a steamboat whistle six hours before they saw it roaring, splashing, steaming and tooting past them. They also easily heard whippoorwills and the caws of blue jays, always too timid to fly over water and flying among or standing upon trees of the banks, too distant to be picked out.

"They are headed to Mr. Livingston's wharf in New Orleans, where he buys timber of any origin with no questions asked. I thought of dragging timber by our tail to New Orleans but decided not to risk our capsizing."

Abraham was afloat on wood unlawfully obtained. He would receive moneys realized by sale of the boat in New Orleans. All men were created equal in being imperfect. None were exempt. And yet — what better use would the Congress make of those timbers? Liberated from Congressional committee disposition, the same timbers could fashion a boat and power the engines of American commerce. In New Orleans the timber would be of much more utility than standing beside a creek somewhere to the North.

CHAPTER FORTY-SEVEN

Abraham admired the beauty of a red-winged blackbird that landed upon the deck briefly, first pecking a crumb, then tilting its head to satisfy its curiosity. When Abraham began to open his mouth to say "hello," the bird flew off. Then an iridescent wonder, like a jewel in air, a ruby-throated hummingbird stared him down before ending their conversation by its own motion. The formerly numerous if not predominant meadowlarks and various sparrows, white-crowned, white-throated, song sparrows, the loons' melancholic, lonesome cries and far more joyful, spirited spring peepers they had heard on the Sangamon, the Illinois, and upper Mississippi down through Arkansas, the chittering chipmunks that had on occasion darted about and whom Johnston had mistaken for field mice were replaced now by a cacophony of bullfrogs making deep ga-lumph sounds over a buzz of cicada tremulos, all nature here seeming like a shaking tambourine. Besides redwings and hummingbirds, bends in the river turned up savannah sparrows and choruses of croaking swamp sparrows now.

Abraham attempted to get the attention of a steamboat chugging upriver, slow but steady. Abraham knew that the steamboat man would sometimes toss over a tied packet of newspapers, but only upon request and only if they were in the mood.

"Paper, please?" Abraham shouted over, his hands at the sides of his mouth.

"All right," a voice said. "Stand clear."

From the deck up above a packet arced with remarkable accuracy — arms used to throwing out and letting down lead to measure depth — and landed with a thud on the bow of the flatboat.

When Abraham opened the packet: nothing but religious tracts.

"See you in Heaven, boy," the same voice boomed, followed by a cackle of vigorous laughter.

Abraham set the packet aside, not knowing but that he might become so hungry for the printed word that he would tear into the tracts. Besides, even if he was not yet that destitute and desperate, they did have a use or two for torn strips of paper.

Later that afternoon, without their realizing until they were fully surrounded, they were in a mass of grinding, variously-shaped logs, some but broken branches, others whole trees, and partly-cut logs. Perhaps a raft of timber had broken up in rapids. Trapped and squeezed between these masses of wood, the boat was in danger of being crushed.

"I say aim for the bank and anchor," Offutt said. "You?" he asked Hanks.

"I figure the same, make for shore slowly, beginning now."

Hanks pointed right with his right hand at the shore closest.

The flatboat, without sails now, moved now by poling on the unyielding and occasionally yielding logs.

"Easy, now, take it slow," Hanks said.

They all eased the boat over and through an unstable, solid sort of river surface. They plowed gradually through the difficulties. Their arms ached long before they reached shore.

"Tie up and wait until the logs pass," Hanks said.

Offutt said, "I agree."

There, tied to trees on a muddy embankment near no obvious plantation they anchored. The log procession, miles long, proceeded as if a forest were parading by, or a glorious, victorious army headed south. Abraham could only think, *this, too, shall pass.* That phrase and then the Voice, *blood coming.*

The logs passed, they cast off and resumed drifting south. Downriver aboard the *Ark*, Offutt played a Latin-speaking, horse-whispering Wizard and Abraham, his grateful apprentice. Offutt blustered about his plans and his stores, including one in New Salem.

Offutt spotted a smoking chimney a good mile away, bragging that he'd smelled it and he wanted some chops and beer. They steered for the shore and, although not with ease and instead by a combined effort of all, managed to hit the edge of the short, squat pier before the tavern. After tying up, they entered the place and took over one of its three tables. Happily, Offutt was right: here were pork chops, as well as fresh bread, meat pies, fruit pies, applesauce, kegs of whiskey and rum, although no beer. They stuffed themselves as if there were to be no tomorrow. They toasted to their survival, to love, and to New Orleans. Abraham drank cider, the rest, rum. The tavern-keeper, a Mr. Wise who hailed originally from Kentucky, could not but be generous with his vacant room and they had a featherbed for free that night. He mentioned his washerwoman, who would wash their shirts in boiling water with lye soap for twenty-cents, two for thirty, could be solicited for additional services for slightly higher fees. Only Johnny was interested, and Hanks discouraged him, whispering a sentence with the word "disease" in it. Abraham volunteered and slept that night aboard the flatboat, lest it be visited in the night by thieves. He took a satchel of an apple, bread and goat cheese. The tavern-keeper gave the rest a spread of biscuits and gravy, goat cheese, bread and goat's milk, which he insisted was a powerful medicine and boon to health. They also had a roasted river sturgeon to eat, maybe five feet when caught, setting on a long wooden truncheon, its moist, white flesh good eating. Everybody filled themselves and, when they hit the featherbed, had no trouble sleeping. The trouble was in getting up early.

CHAPTER FORTY-EIGHT

Once underway, walking when the sun was well up, they noticed the little herd of tavern goats, two butting each other in the head while others ate what looked like maggoty meat. Johnny puked while Hanks and Offutt stood by, arms akimbo, laughing.

Abraham left them to manage now while he read. They were getting closer to Natchez and roads beside the river were busier than any roads they had known in Illinois, Indiana or Kentucky. Shiny black-painted carriages with fringe tops and fine wheels with thin spokes highlighted a parade of horses of all kinds, some ridden by gentlemen with top hats and handkerchiefs about their lower faces as shields against the dust, ladies side-saddled, farmer's wagons, carts of all kinds, some large and heavy ones hauled by teams of oxen, along with foot travelers of all ages, both genders, alone, in groups, with baskets, or carrying guns. Abraham never could get over the sight of hummingbirds twice the size of wrens buzzing like bees up and down, darting around magnolia trees and sucking the honey from the trees' blossoms. Bales of cotton in incredible sizes and numbers suddenly began to pop up here and there along the river, sometimes covered, always watched by people, white or black, until a rendezvous would take the cotton away, probably to New Orleans, from there as often as not to mills in England. This river was a conduit of international commerce at this point. Prosperity stamped its banks now with clearings, spacious green fields populated by cows, sometimes fine horses and colts, sheep by the hundreds, regular lines of tall trees, mostly pines. Man and not Nature was planting hereabouts. Broad avenues fringed by stately trees offered an approach comically grand compared to what it led to, but the avenues reflected these settlers' hopes. Nor were they unreasonable to hope. True, poor wooden huts persisted in appearing but so also now pillared, white-washed mansions proudly faced this river. Banks and other building completely of red brick dotted the shores as well. No doubt, jails were needed, and courthouses, printers, post offices and stores as well as boardinghouses and churches of every denomination. However, Abraham noticed, the buildings topped by steeples or beside graveyards were never the best buildings in these towns.

Here, on the outskirts of each town or village, carrion crows did the work of cleaning the bodies, eating flesh down to the bones of animals, horses, cows, goats, dogs, cats, all of the rot the town or village produced under the sun. The work of man ended and the work of crows began once the carcass was dumped into these ditches.

The crew on the flatboat rarely ate together, being hungry and free at different times. The kitchen was small, the quarters were tight. The best things they found here they simply roasted in glowing embers by plucking and hacking to pieces the duck, the teal, the fish or (most preferred) the partridge and placing pieces in the heat for a time, determining by nose when the pieces were done, pieces then set to cool and to be available for anyone to grab and eat on the fly. Such meat was always chewy but it served. The best meat they purchased with a few minutes of sign language upon encountering an Indian waving from shore. He tossed them a twenty-pound tom turkey and asked for and got in return a silver dollar. Besides the meals, Abraham made himself some quill pens.

They shared a buffalo skin in rotation as their best sleeping accommodation, although Offutt most often claimed that it was his turn and from his decree there was no appeal.

CHAPTER FORTY-NINE

It was a boon to be alive and conscious. For Abraham, the Mississippi by night was a matter of profound wonder. It was unimaginable that people slept, living down here on the banks of this river. Why were they not out to see the stars? Why did they not, or their children at least, hunt fireflies? Drifting along with the current on a calm, clear night was as great a blessing as Abraham ever received.

Abraham alone saw the passing steamboat. At first a distant and silent swarm of fireflies, the steamboat came up river gradually and more grandly than in daylight, chugging ever louder, its sidewheels digging into the water and splashing the Mississippi noisily behind it. As it passed, it was a huge behemoth that seemed to belch fire, a great orange glow, sparking from atop its tall stacks. It was a sight to behold, once seen, never forgot. So few were awake and alert for such miracles.

There was the rare traveler, perhaps a doctor, perhaps a midwife, maybe a pastor, each mile or so on the bank or in the crest of hills above. Abraham would see the shine of a lantern, often swaying, attached to a carriage. Gentry, surely. Here, floating as if over the stars, reflected on water and as present below his chin as over his head, star-struck, Abraham passed the night without haste. He almost regretted the pink hues and streaks of dawn when it came over on the left horizon. The day could not be so awesome as the night, the night of the stars.

Some days, they halted and Offutt led Hanks or Johnny or both — but never Abraham — out with the shotguns to try their luck. In Arkansas and Mississippi thick vines, thorny green briars, cane breaks and high rushes soon entangled any path. The ground was always giving way underfoot, soft mud or swampy soil. Sometimes they brought back a hare or two, once a young deer, but most often it was birds. Three times they came back with hatfuls of delicious strawberries, fresh, flavorful raspberries and pinkish-orange berries that Offutt called "the grandest huckleberries you will ever see," sour sorry specimens that did not seem even ripe.

CHAPTER FIFTY

On the Mississippi side now, Offutt had them stop at a well-kept, broad pier. It led to a store around which piles of barrels and bales of cotton stood so that it resembled a Medieval fortress. Inside, the storekeeper filled two sacks with goods for them, a small bag of good, fresh-milled, fine white flour, a smallish wheel of yellow cheese, new apples and potatoes, carrots and onions. Lastly, Offutt purchased two venison hams for fifty cents. They could all but smell a savory stew ahead.

Offutt also purchased powder and cast lead balls for their guns, which the storekeeper selected and boxed and wrapped for them. He was a very neat man, and a slow man, but they enjoyed the leisure that his store offered, and within it a vicarious prosperity. Butcher knives in a glass case looked good but were expensive, as was the assortment of firearms, new and used, up on the wall around the mounted head of a twelve-point buck. Abraham spent a few coins on a small bottle of ink and a few sheets of paper. He already had turkey quill pens aboard. Abraham reminded Offutt of candles, which might easily have been forgotten.

"Yes, we may as well, let there be light, writing love letters," Offutt said.

As they clomped out with their filled sacks, Johnny whooping and hollering, holding up over his head his treasures, powder and balls for the guns. They were clomping noisily on the wooden landing, as if timed, a great steam whistle startled them and the river churned as the *General Shelby* came passing by their review. All hands of that three-story steamboat seeming to stand at attention before them. Passengers on each deck looked at them, some waved, including pretty ladies. Johnny went crazy waving back until Offutt told him to cut it. No longer whopping, they then got aboard their own humble, smelly, silent craft.

It was quite warm, muggy as they left the landing. They heard relief distantly, claps of thunder. They had not been afloat again five minutes before rain began coming in sheets. They could not see but a few feet ahead and the noise of rain on the water was deafening, they had to shout to one another no matter how close they stood. They continued, thinking, as turned out to be correct, that this was a summer storm that would pass and the sun would come out in a matter of minutes.

Hanks said, "Nothing like that could last long. No more than a man and a maid in their throes."

149

"And a pity that is," Offutt said, laughing, baring the gap between his big two front teeth.

Abraham was reminded of a story that he then told, one he shared with Johnston without embarrassment now, a boy no longer. It seemed that a certain mademoiselle from France came to live in New Orleans, where a wealthy planter took her on as a maid for his wife and as a seamstress.

The time came, the planter needed a new pair of pants himself and he asked the new maid if she knew how to make pants.

Her English was not good, so she said, "I know not vat dat ees."

He pointed toward his legs and gestured, "This is pants."

The young lady thereupon blushed and said, "Dat I care not much for, monsieur."

CHAPTER FIFTY-ONE

They spent the night in rain, mid-river.

The next morning dawned clear but hot. Butterflies by the thousands flew over the boat, like so much fluttering yellow paper or ribbons in the air. It was unreal, as in a dream, to stand at the bow of their little boat and look ahead into the swarm over, beside and before them, a dense pack that had a peculiar odor, almost a sweet smell, of dry fruit perhaps, or very faint pressed flowers.

"Lucky they're not bees," Hanks said. "Or bats."

They had had close encounters with both swarms of bees and, once upon a twilight, with streams of an astonishing number of bats. They did not then or in memory relish their near contact with either species.

An Indian squaw and two young ones were out from the bank in the edge of the river, apparently preparatory to bathing, as they came by mid-stream. She and the children bore expressionless interest in them and their odd flatboat as it went by, in a perfectly natural and unfeigned simplicity of manner. Did they know sorrow? Abraham had no doubt that they did, but only the sadness that comes from real and direct disaster, not the artificial worry and anxiety that afflicts the white man, who may go into a rage or burst into tears for a report of plunging cotton prices in London. The squaw looked at them and, somewhat absently, reached up under one arm and, they reckoned, itched and detached a large louse that she thereupon cracked with the obvious gestures incidental to cracking. Abraham laughed, not at the squaw but at the story he recalled of the woman who cracked lice as her husband drowned her.

Peach and apple trees, past blossom and now into the phase of small fruit, were common along the banks. Spanish beard clung to branches of tall cypress and cottonwood trees. Pelicans, for the first time, flapped wings overhead, seeming by size variations to be adults escorting their young ones back to the Gulf.

On prior flatboats the custom was to get blankets and sleep upon the top deck, as it were. This flatboat's top deck was new timber and still oozing with sap. That left the idea open of sleeping below decks. That accounted for the design of a scuttle hole, with a homemade ladder, to these quarters. The place of storage of their victuals and bedding smelled notwithstanding, given the smells of greasy cooking and of their animals, notwithstanding John Johnston's dutiful attention to duty, insofar as he had a nose, too. Even in a spot at the stern end, where Offutt originally intended a table for himself and charts, when they had cleared and stacked cargo to provide a sort of cozy nest, no door blocked the noises and smells of the hogs. Nobody had much relief from the smells, night or day. Sometimes they dreamed of flower gardens. That was their relief.

Up above, Hanks rigged a thin plank as a sort of mast for cloth sails, backed on both sides by broad planks to act as added sails. The broad planks came down and stayed down on the top deck any time the winds were of no avail, which was half the trip. Their boat caught the eye of many individual on the banks. People in Beardstown hooted and hollered, families brought out the old folks to see the sight. Offutt only wished out loud that he had been able to charge for admission.

"We'd play to a packed house," he said.

CHAPTER FIFTY-TWO

One time on his first trip with Allen Gentry, Abraham had heard a riverboat chugging and a holler. By the acoustics of the river just where only the steamboat and their small flatboat occupied space, Abraham heard, "Go outside to the left of the first snag above the point, inside to the right the next one."

To navigate the river with which he was unfamiliar, to hear someone on another vessel speak confidently with such obvious mastery of where to sail, was discouraging. What they were doing was going "point to point." This was groping. Boatmen were finding their way a few steps at a time. They all seemed uncertain of anything but what they could see, relying less on memory, and certainly on no book.

That entire first trip with another novice, Allen Gentry, was a long voyage without a constitution. This second trip, Abraham knew more. He was among men, Offutt and Hanks, who had several trips' worth of experience but not down the Mississippi. On board, Abraham was master of the Mississippi and he piloted point to point. Abraham was relaxed only when anchored or ashore, not afloat. Afloat, he was not as nervous as he had been three years earlier, but he was still nervous.

Offutt came forward to the bow on an errand. Unbuttoning and taking a leak into the Mississippi, his cigar a red star clenched in his teeth as he took aim and let fly a great arc.

Done, he let out one great, echoing whoop.

To Abraham, he said, "Noisy, ain't I?"

Abraham said, "You are noisy. You always been so?"

"Here," Offutt said, seeing a pier and a giant slave waving a red bandanna. "Someone wishes to trade. Does it look right to you?"

Abraham, his hand up to his forehead to see more clearly, taking a long moment scanning the trees and bushes all along the shore before answering, then said, "Looks like he's alone. I think we could chance it."

He rowed the flatboat, a task in his hands that appeared easier than it was, getting the boat up over to the pier as the current seemed intent upon grabbing and carrying the boat faster and further down river than that destination. Abraham, and only Abraham, tied the cable to link the boat to shore. He did not trust any other to wrap loosely enough not to snap, and not too loose either, but just in the right range between loose and tight. Nor did he actually cease his glances up and along the shore for any sign of others. Near shore, they were fair game if a gang jumped them. They could be carrying more than clubs this time.

"What have we, Rastus?" Offutt asked, using any old name for the slave, as was customary.

Not coming closer, betraying suspicions of his own, "Sir, have you bacon?" he bellowed through cupped hands. A lone slave might be seized and bound and sold down river as easily as any White man might be robbed. Abraham found a degree of relief in the slave's nervous stance. This man was large-boned and tall but he carried his hands up above his waist and his knees were a bit bent, like a man prepared to run at the sight of a lasso tossed. Such things had doubtless happened and never been known outside of the few involved.

Offutt reared back and, dropping his voice almost inaudibly now, said, "No need to shout, my man. Bacon we have, but only the best and most select, well-smoked and tasty cuts. Fit for the New Orleans table. I do not know if you would care to meet my price."

"What is your price, master?" the giant asked, less loudly now, not to appear anxious and increase the asking price.

"Well, Rastus, a dollar a side, prime cut, smoked and sugar-cured," Offutt said. "Three sides for two-and-a-half. In good coin. No banknotes, no promissory notes."

The slave, who had twice that stashed away under a rock a hundred feet away, said that he would tell the master if the gentlemen would wait. Offutt agreed to "tarry here another five minutes."

The slave seemed to run off at great speed. He soon and silently disappeared in the overgrown bushes and trees, through which they could see the lights of a big house beyond. A rich plantation, probably — if not indebted. But they were all indebted. Crickets chirped, cicadas trilled and for a few minutes neither man said anything. Then, Offutt spoke.

"I should have said a dollar-and-a-half per side, five dollars for three," Offutt said, adding a lesson point for his student, "but coinage, *specie*, is something in itself. A banknote may be worth nothing. What do you think of the river? Is it different the second time?"

Abraham looked back at it.

"It's a wonder any time. A geologist must tell me but I think it was flowing when Columbus came looking, no, when Christ suffered on the cross —"

"When Moses was wandering the desert, Lincoln, when Adam came up out of the clay, then and now, this river flowed," Offutt said.

"Is that not a wonder? Older than the first man, still strong, still fresh, never dried, never frozen, never sleeps, never rests, onward, ever onward."

"Where's that boy gone to?" Offutt asked.

Abraham felt a twinge of concern as if the slave's absence meant some malicious plotting and preparation, but only a twinge. Even so, he knew where a pick handle was and how far from an ax he stood.

"What's going on?" Hanks asked, his head poking up. "Trouble?"

As soon as he hauled himself up out of the hold and stood atop the deck, Johnny scooted up above deck as well, asking why they had stopped. The boat usually only stopped well after sunset, using each minute of daylight, twilight and hardly-see light to make progress toward New Orleans.

"We got a deal cooking," Offutt said. "Why don't you two get down in the hold and find three sides of bacon?"

CHAPTER FIFTY-THREE

The slave heard "Rastus" from these men without hearing more than their ignorance. After the last sale, on his fourth river farm, he was lately dubbed "Cicero." Cicero, however, could remember his name from his mama. It had been Tiger. Since then, beginning age twelve, he had gone through three plantations and three names and, by any name, he was going to outfox the foxes. He turned over the rock and took up the coins he would use. This was not for master, this was his own trade. It was for his Nance and their baby daughters.

Master thought Cicero was on his way to the next plantation. Let him think so. And these white folk on the boat, well, he took satisfaction in his idea of bargaining. It was that more than the bacon itself that pleased him. He was not going to come back with quite three dollars. The white man's prices were too high, anyway. Tiger knew what Tiger knew.

The giant returned, shouting ahead of himself, "I have the money, master."

"Three dollars?" Offutt said, his arm over Abraham's wrist, not to stir just yet.

"Master said three sides, sir, if you please, sir. I got a two-dollar gold piece and silver."

Offutt tapped Abraham's wrist, waved and nodded to the slave that Abraham would row to shore.

In counting on the pier next, Offutt had a decision to make. The slave only brought a two-dollar coin and three dimes. Would it suffice? It would. Offutt had no doubt that he had the best of the bargain. This side of bacon in New Orleans would not go for half of this handful of coins.

Offutt kept the proffered coins. He had Abraham heft up and hand over the bundle to the slave up on the pier. Although the slave took time to unfold the cloth, to see and smell the bacon, he did not tarry longer in conversation. After inhaling deeply, and making a noise signifying pleasure, he cradled the side of bacon in its greasy gunny sack.

Offutt nodded to Abraham and, back and seated again, they set off again.

Offutt was moved to sing:

In vain we lavish out our lives
To gather empty wind:
The choicest blessings earth can yield
Will starve a hungry mind

"That don't rhyme worth a damn, but your hungry mind reminded me of it, Abe," Offutt said. "Ain't we something, riding down this river. I suppose someday they'll build bridges and the day of flatboats and steamboats will be at an end. But for now, we are kings. I am, thus, being rowed by royalty and traveling in high style."

In the shade, by the river, as he took steps, the slave watched the white men rowing to their flatboat, singing and talking. As Tiger watched, the tall younger man made graceful motions with the pole. He was a strong man, Tiger thought. Holding the side of bacon, Tiger felt a restfulness strange to him, foreign and inexplicable.

The flatboat itself next floated away, smaller by the minute in his sight.

Then water was all he could see, the Mississippi that he had lived by all of his days.

The boat, with the men, was gone.

Surely, they were going to New Orleans, where Tiger himself had once been sold at Hewlett's Exchange. It was a riverside auction house run by gentlemen in frilly shirts and tall hats, one wearing gold button jackets with wide lapels who sold him. He was only twelve then but bid up to three-hundred dollars.

CHAPTER FIFTY-FOUR

Later that night, Abraham and Offutt on the upper deck, Hanks and Johnny below in the cabin, Offutt asked Abraham, "You asleep?"

"No," Abraham said. "But not awake either."

"Well, wake then, prince, and view the stars, they are in a glorious array for your amusement," Offutt said. "The profit of a day was already made before Spears ever appeared. Imagine it, bacon for eighty cents a side."

"A lot more than it fetches in Illinois," Abraham said. "But money may get our throats cut. Did you think we brought aboard an honest man?"

Abraham had become captain. He was living up to the title and offering advice and suggestions to Offutt, not timidly, either. Offutt noticed and responded seriously. He said, "I think we brought aboard a man who wants to get to New Orleans and out of the country without showing his face in Natchez or any spot along the banks, that's what I think."

"We think alike."

Abraham sat up and, his arms crossed over his knees atop the thin, raggedy blanket, looked up. The stars twinkled against a black velvet sky. It was unearthly quiet even for the mid-river, and the boat floated palpably but in near-complete darkness, bottom-of-well darkness.

"Different than daytime," Abraham said after a long minute.

"You signed on with me to make money," Offutt said. It went a long distance to make all of his decisions understandable, if not wise.

"Well," Abraham said, "I'm going along, ain't I?"

Offutt waxed philosophical for this one night anyway.

"Don't chase after lucre and gain. 'The love of money is the root of all evil,'" Offutt said, being this night of nights one of two men atop a flatboat looking up at stars.

Abraham understood and wanted Offutt to understand that he understood. Under twinkling stars or not, Abraham said, "I need money to make any progress in life, Denton."

"Don't chase after it is all I am saying. Let it chase you."

"What do you mean? If you mean anything. Are you funning?"

"Never more serious. Chasing after money, lives go off track pretty quick, whether they succeed in getting any money or not," Offutt said. "Money is not the destination, Abraham, it's the journey. You thought you were headed to New Orleans to make the first bit of your fortune."

"I'm not?"

"You are. That's what worries me. I see you every day doing your trading, counting your money —"

"I didn't know you could see," Abraham said.

"Hear you, more like. I hear the clink of the coins," Offutt said.

"I'll be quieter when my money's in notes," Abraham said. "I'll just rustle then, no more clinking."

"You joke but this is how it is, how you are just now. You are facing a lifetime ahead and I want you to have a good one, possibly a great one. When you can — I say, when you can —leave money behind as your goal and link your name with some cause bigger than you are."

"Go into politics?" Abraham asked.

"Did I say politics?" Offutt asked.

"Was that not intended by 'big causes'?"

"It could be. It could be inventions. It could be, praise the Lord, preaching."

"I think you meant politics. You saw a politician in me."

"Why, would that tickle you?"

"It might."

"Then, you run for the legislature when you get the chance. If Posey the storekeeper can win, you can win. I'll set you up a store in New Salem just like his. Maybe you could get your friend Jackson to name you the postmaster. And read all the newspapers and get to talk with everybody."

"The ones that come by for mail and have none are always ready for talk."

"That they are. You can tell your jokes, even the old ones will seem new."

A time went by under the stars.

"Politics? Seriously, Offutt?" Abraham asked.

"By the stars above, yes, Abraham. Politics. You're no hand at making money so you'd best make other plans."

They both laughed.

CHAPTER FIFTY-FIVE

For a long time, they were both silent. Then Offutt said, "New Salem is on my list."

This was the first Abraham heard of any list.

"What list?" he asked.

Offutt cut loose. He said, "Of stores. I'm going to have stores and boats. Toll bridges, too, and riverboats and stages. I'll break the horses in, that'll be my only job. Breaking in horses and counting the money."

Lincoln said, straddling teasing and being serious, "You're chasing money."

"I have nothing more or better in me. I read and write but I don't read and write like you, my man. Don't just piddle it away, writing against the Bible—"

"I make sense."

"You do, but it's not a great cause."

Offutt had spoiled the mood.

"You're quiet," Offutt said after a bit.

"I am," Abraham said.

"Thinking?"

"Yes."

"Then think about this: never scoff at anybody's religion. Leave religion be, and God, too."

"I read the Bible," Abraham said, with a defensive tone.

"Read the Bible the way you do, the way you take it. The Bible will do you plenty of good and no harm. I know you and I know the Bible. You are not enemies, but friends. But leave the Bible aside. It is beyond the Bible that you set your sights."

"And just how do you know that, sir?"

"I've seen and met and dined with DeWitt Clinton. He's like you."

"DeWitt Clinton?"

The Governor of New York was most famous for building the Erie Canal. Many considered him greater than Jackson for that feat, joining isolated upstate farmers into commerce with the country. To be compared with DeWitt Clinton was exhilirating. It made his toes turn just to think of that.

Sitting back, his arms behind his head, looking up at the stars in this dream of a night, Abraham asked, "What's he like?"

Offutt stood up, fished a cigar up out of his pocket and lit up. Then, after a few puffs, holding the railing of the flatboat, looking out on the Mississippi, his words flowed into Abraham's ears.

"He's just like you, puts his pants on one leg at a time. He watches to see what he might do with help, and he looks for help. I see that is how to become great."

Abraham said, "I should like to make a mark. I should like to be esteemed."

He was dissatisfied, overhearing himself and his squeakish voice, a voice lost in the vastness of the night on the Mississippi.

Offutt said, "You could do as much, Abe, to make the Sangamon navigable."

"I was planning on going back to Indiana and —"

"You need two plans."

"Two plans?"

"One for yourself and one for the outside."

"What do you mean?"

"For yourself, hunker down and pull in, man yourself, gird your loins, don't say anything to anybody, trust nobody and no one, give them no idea or clue but inward, plot your course. Be the most shut-mouthed man ever lived."

"No jokes and stories?"

"All jokes and stories, nothing but jokes and stories. You be the same jolly man anybody is pleased to see coming, like Posey. He told me about your first, gave me your crack louse joke. I still laugh."

"That was a good one."

"But your other plan, for the world, you can give that, you have to, you sell the world you want to live in. Take it up. See it, taste it, talk about it, write it. Patience and a plan with a long time horizon will get you there."

"Did that get DeWitt Clinton to where he is?" Abraham asked.

Offutt was not in a mood to answer directly, it soon appeared. He readily quoted whatever he had said to DeWitt Clinton over their dinner. It did not seem that he had much to quote of what DeWitt Clinton said to him. No matter, until they stopped conversing and went to bed, Offutt shared his memories and opinions (more opinions than memories) of DeWitt Clinton, Governor of New York and the inventor, if you will, of the Erie Canal.

CHAPTER FIFTY-SIX

A trading scow from Indiana came by, moving slightly faster than the *Ark*. The farmer, traveling with his pipe-smoking wife and three curious little ones, all eyes, big eyes, had a shipment of chairs and pumpkins. In a short two minutes of conversation, the weather looked good, they agreed. Plantations ahead, richer the closer they came to the city, might take some chairs and pumpkins. They wished the Hoosier luck.

Abraham thought about bridges, and the kind of structure a bridge required.

"Ice floes would be hard on a bridge. But maybe they could build of stone and iron and keep a bridge in place," Abraham said. "But if they did that, they would still have to allow for boats, even steamboats, a way to get under and go about their lawful business."

"Why? The man wants to build a bridge, it is his right," Offutt said.

"Not fully, not entirely. He must work within what is, and steamboats were in place and using the river lawfully before the bridge man came," Abraham said. "I believe that the law will protect the steamboat from harm. The bridge man will have to make allowances."

"You are a smart one, Abe," Offutt said. "Ever considered becoming a merchant?"

"Not particularly, no, Denton," Abraham said.

Offutt began to sing:

Without money
Come to Jesus Christ and buy

He broke off then and asked, "You recall where we hung up on the lip of the dam, that village on the Sangamon with the mill and that gal you put your eye on?"

"New Salem."

"New Salem exactly. I'm going to open a store right exactly in New Salem. You could operate it for me. I saw how that little mill draws folks from all around for the grinding. You know what I did?"

"What did you do?" Abraham asked.

"I bought that mill," he said. "Got a deed, and gave my promissory note to Rutledge, he's the one with that pretty daughter. He has big plans for New Salem. It's a boomtown."

"And now you own the mill?" Abraham asked.

"Mill and a store that Rutledge is contracting to build for me right now in the town square, opposite of his tavern. While folks pass through that village, they would like to buy something, and they have money to do the buying, but without me there is no mercantile establishment to serve their need. Am I right, sir?"

Abraham, smiling too broadly, caught up with Offutt's "mercantile establishment" talk, said, "No, not until they get home."

"Home, sir? Will you listen to the boy? Why make these good people wait as they struggle homeward, when their needs might be served in this New Salem, this bound-to-grow-to-glory storied town? And mark the river, over which we flew as if we had wings. The Sangamon River can surely support a boat going out and back. Oh, it's a perfect place. New Salem."

Abraham had not heard enough about himself in this great speech.

"You were thinking of me becoming a merchant, Mr. Offutt?" he asked.

"You, Abe? You. Why, I could see a smart man like you running my store at New Salem, as my agent, my *major domo*, my acting representative for all matters of buying and selling, my attorney on the premises. You at the very head, the top rung of a mercantile establishment. The man in charge, the deciding vote in every matter before you. What do you say? Would you not like that?"

"What would you pay me?"

Offutt made a face as if he had just eaten something rotten or sour.

"Pay? Why, Abraham, I am not offering a mere job to a clerk, what I have in my hands is a partnership — a partnership in a growing enterprise, an opportunity, your best chance of getting on and up in this world. And of seeing your gal every day."

"She is not my gal and I cannot live on nothing."

"You will not live on nothing. You will be rich. No man who has ever partnered with me has failed to become rich, this trip of ours to New Orleans being but an initial evidence and installment of that process of tapping into this country's great wealth and untold riches."

"I go on commission?"

"You have a head on your shoulders. I must congratulate you for hitting the nail on the *tte*, as the Frenchman said. Yes, a liberal commission. What do you guess? Just guess. Go ahead. One per cent? One-and-one-half?"

"Five?"

"Abraham, I shall not profit five per cent myself, no one does regularly in retail enterprise, this is an inviolable law of commerce. I shall be lucky, lucky indeed — but I often and often am so lucky — as to obtain two per cent profits."

"What is my share of this two cents?"

"Why, my son, I shall give that entire two per cent to you, in the first year. Just to get us started and knowing one another on a friendly basis, as trusting friends who do not intend to part before we are rich. As the business improves, as the village grows, as this river trade center develops, the boats docking and unloading, then loading up again with a frequency that is astonishing to consider, a marvel merely to estimate, why, you shall by then enjoy three per cent and I shall have a poor one per cent. But it will make us both rich because what we lack in per cent, we shall make up for in volume. You know arithmetic? The tables?"

"I do some ciphering," Abraham said. "Looks like a storm."

He pointed to Offutt the scudding start of a darkening horizon.

"I see," Offutt said. "Well, perhaps I should duck under and nap. I go, Abe. Should the storm arrive and last some hours, are you all right doing the rowing while I sleep or shall I summon young Johnston?"

"I will be fine."

As Offutt curled up unseen under the deck, a man who slept when his head but touched the round of his folded coat, Abraham thought about New Salem. Two per cent was two dollars for every hundred. Say a thousand dollars passed through his hands in a year. Twenty dollars, but nothing to pay for shelter, work out the food and clothing next. He would not really be rich but he would not be a farmer either. And he would see this Ann Rutledge again. If she liked books, wouldn't that be something? Somebody in that village would like reading. He would have friends. He would very much like to have educated friends like Brown and Reed. And twenty dollars. Idly, Pa's words came to mind. *When you make a bad bargain, hug it the tighter.*

As it rained steadily, lightning flashing and rumbles of thunder in the distance, observing the constant flow of this broad and deep river, ceaseless since before the time of Christ, night and day, inexhaustibly flowing, flowing to the sea, Abraham's ever-curious mind sent and sent again in awe and in wonder with no answer: *Where does all the water come from?*

CHAPTER FIFTY-SEVEN

At one pier there was a barge already tied up and their arrival at dusk led to a joint meal aboard that larger craft. It turned out the crew were lumbermen filling the hold with red-star sweet gum planks from trees they felled and milled ashore nearby.

"We also got firewood from the tupelos around here," the captain-foreman said as they ate rice, pork, peas, along with bitter coffee and slightly rancid fruit pies. The cabin of the barge was roomy enough but sticky and resin-smelling like a split pine, as well as smoky from the fire and strong on pork in the air from cooking that frequently. No harm, it was close and homey — and, just like home, full of flies. Nobody felt far in the woods or far from home in this barge, as on their frail flatboat in the middle of the river.

"Tell you, some of the red-stars go up over a hundred feet and more than three feet around. They are tough to bring down," the captain said.

"But down we bring 'em," a crewman said, to a chorus. Nobody stood on ceremony, every man had his voice or opinion. This was an energetic group. Abraham realized how Hanks, Johnny, Offutt and he, comparatively, were life-less slugs.

"The tallest ones go back well before the white man set his foot on this continent, years before Columbus captured the first slave," the captain said.

Abraham weighed in his mind the picture of a young man, the crewman of Captain Columbus, sneaking around a half-grown red-star tree with a rope lariat, spotting a likely native, a young boy, bringing him down and hog-tying him and sailing back with him to Spain, taking his life, stealing him from himself. He stopped eating the pie.

The captain noticed and said, "Sorry. We were going to chuck it but sometimes hunger makes the best sauce. Don't eat what you don't want. We give it to the pigs."

As if on call, there was a ruckus of squeals back out in the increasingly dark woods beyond the pier ashore. The pigs were active, fighting or mating or something. The foreman went on about their occupation and their current project and how far along they were now. Although from other states originally (Tennessee, Mississippi and Alabama), they were now Arkansans with families in Arkansas waiting on them to head for New Orleans once the barge was full, a project of a few more weeks, "given fair weather and no accidents." He told of losing one crewman the prior season to a snake bite that got infected. He "blew up like a balloon, and then turned black until he stopped breathing alto-gether." One of the crewman said, with satisfaction, "We got the snake, slit him and salted him and fed him to the hogs." Offutt had a boxful of samples, as he always did, and spoke highly of other "premium merchandise" he could be per-suaded for a price to part with but this group was not of that mind. They had no interest in trading for the buttons, needles, thread and other sundries the plan-tations usually traded for at premium. "Our wives have more than they need," the foreman said, "we don't want to spoil 'em."

Offutt said at least to take something for the food they'd shared.

"Oh, do not insult our generosity, gentlemen travelers. Fellow pilgrims, what we have we share," the foreman told Offutt. "Just like the old Christians, holding our table to break bread with our neighbors."

"Brothers," Offutt said by way of a one-word prelude to singing a hymn for them about the Popish lady. It was the foulest one in the hymnbook and it set the tone for the rest of their visit. They admired stories that Abraham came up with to tell, several of the smuttiest ever to be presented at a Christian table. Hanks and John felt warm and comfortable, full and so sleepy that they were disinclined to take part in the patter. The evening ended when rain began and Offutt decided they'd best care for the pigs aboard the flatboat and be sure of the safety of their craft during the storm.

Aboard that night, rain battering the roof, the river rocking the flatboat in the wind, Abraham heard snoring but could not close his own eyes. How pitiful the plans of men and women are, as noble, venerable trees that had stood before the white man went into cords of firewood sold cheaply, and enslavement con-tinued apace to grip millions since Columbus's time. The net misery of this pro-gressing world was increasing. His sister, Sally, came to mind. God, after having allowed her to become merry and full-sailed, so pleased and happy as a mother-to-be, and dreaming dreams that he could see in her eyes and delighted to see, God let the babe drop from her womb dead.

The next day, laid out in a pine coffin, in her white wedding dress, inex-plicably rust-stained or yellow-colored.

On the flatboat he was breathing. Abraham was on the river. God was observant of them all. It was written that not a sparrow falls but God notes it. *The implication of this text,* Abraham almost mimicked aloud, *brothers and sisters, is that God likewise notes when we fail and when we succeed, when we sin and when we decline to yield to temptation.* It only says that He notices when we die. He notices when one of the sparks goes out, cold, dark. No more than that.

Did not Jesus himself teach, "Let your speech be 'Aye, aye,' or 'Nay, nay,' as more than this is from the Devil?" Be plain, be honest. So no more than this:

God knows and notices when you die. What you take with you is the shroud they bury you in, or the stained dress. What you leave is the big thing, what you have done to make people remember that you have lived, and what your name was. Would anyone remember Abraham Lincoln if he died today? No. That saddened him. Other men might not care at all but that saddened him. It never grieved Pa, the blind, dancing bear, now daughterless, but it grieved his son.

I'll bring the entire tribe of Lincolns up out of the dirt and known and celebrated. By the sheer force of what I shall do.

Abraham found no bottom under his pole as the flatboat drifted out past the muddy shoals. What shall I do?

Abraham recalled the night of the attack, that wild scuffle when he held a club in his hand, murder in his heart, bleeding from his head, blinding his eyes. Those other men's faces, their eyes bore into him. He wanted to kill none, not even those who had set upon him to kill him.

Underneath, without words, in their eyes, Abraham thought he saw the flicker, from their eyes to his, of a mutual recognition.

CHAPTER FIFTY-EIGHT

The storm passed and Offutt sang:

> *Zion, afflicted with wave upon wave,*
> *Whom no man can comfort, whom no man can save;*
> *With darkness surrounding, with terrors dismayed,*
> *In toiling and rowing thy strength is decayed.*
> *Loud roaring, the billows now night overwhelm,*
> *But skillful's the pilot who sits at the helm;*
> *His wisdom conducts thee, his power thee defends,*
> *In safety and quiet they warfare he ends.*

"Point to point, Abe," Offutt said. "We are staying the course point to point, guided landmark by landmark, no further than we can see. The boatmen all go point by point and that's the safest way."

They continued to watch the lightning fade in the distance. Now, a Negro came out from the bank ahead and threw or dipped a scoop net over and over. He stood at a point where the river formed an eddy, from which in a few minutes, as they saw, he harvested several tolerably large catfish.

Below Natchez, at about Baton Rouge, the river was smoother, deeper waters, much more free of sawyers and snags. The plantations on the banks were increasing in number and closer together. Here, there were many landings, some with flatboats. A surer, higher profit than in New Orleans could be obtained here by regular callers, but strangers would have trouble getting in on the trade. They drifted by, content with the hope of New Orleans prices.

Standing atop the forecabin, both hands up over his eyes, Indian scout-style, to see better, Johnny yelled to come look at the roses. A huge garden of red, yellow and white roses were all in bloom. He yelled that, beyond them, he could see cane fields and they went on forever.

"You see any cuckoos, other than yourself?" Offutt yelled back from below. He was cooking chops and beans, tasting as he did.

Offutt and Abraham got to talking over chops.

"Abraham's a Biblical name," Offutt said.

"I'm named for my grandfather, my father's father."

"You ever meet him?"

"He was killed by Indians."

"Where was this?"

"Bucks County, Pennsylvania."

"Your father was orphaned, half-orphaned then."

"He was. He was the youngest son but he saved one brother from a savage who was waving a tomahawk over his head and yelling."

"Brave boy."

"He had a rifle he knew how to fire. Just before he brought it down, Pa said he aimed for the heart, where the Indian had a charm hanging. Not a lucky charm."

Not much could top that story. Offutt gave advice instead.

"Deep breaths, strong sweats, big appetites and regular bowels make for a happy and healthy life. You ever read the Bible?"

"Enough for me," Abraham said.

Up above, Johnny was calling out that they come and look, look at a grove of orange trees. Hanks was up there looking, neither Offutt nor Abraham moved.

Hereabouts, closer to cities, gigs and horsemen here all seemed to vie with one another as in a race, making all possible speed. They may not have been intent upon any particular destination, but they made dust.

Before Johnny and Hanks, lizards, frogs, water snakes and alligators all came into sight, as did huge cotton fields.

In the stern cabin, Offutt said, "I don't believe in religion myself. I think religions are ways of making money off of poor folk. The best thing about it is the Bible."

Abraham said, "I think there's no book like it, but I can find a fault on every page."

"How so, Abe?"

"How Joshua stopped the sun so they had light to battle the Ammorites. If he did that, why, we'd have all flown off into the sky. God making the world in seven days, and Noah's boat having room for two of all animals."

"Oho, Abe, now the boatman comes forth of you. But maybe Noah's boat was bigger than this one."

"Boat still had to float. With the animals and their fodder and food for about six months? The Bible says one boat. An ark big enough for all the animal pairs and fodder and food would sink under their weight. If it was smaller, the animals would not fit, or their provender."

"Then how did the human race survive the Great Flood?" Offutt asked.

"The same way we survived the Deep Snow," Abraham said, "by the skin of our teeth."

CHAPTER FIFTY-NINE

They were talking again, just Abraham and Offutt, atop the flatboat under a star-filled sky. Offutt was repeating some of the same advice he had already given to Abraham.

"I saw a shooting star," Abraham said.

"Where?"

"Over your head as you said not to chase money."

"An omen."

"Maybe. I was thinking of making a little money first, though, before freeing all the slaves. I kind of feel like a slave on this boat, no offense, Mister Offutt."

"Take up your opportunities in Illinois. Here, I'll make it easy for you to court that Ann Rutledge you kept making eyes at and who was no less interested herself in you. You be my manager of the store I set up in New Salem."

"I don't know."

"You do know. Where's those shooting stars? Nothing over my head when I say the name 'Ann Rutledge'?"

In fact, although Abraham had been hoping for just that, no shooting star appeared overhead upon just that name. He felt badly about it but not so bad it stopped him from giving a reply to Offutt.

"Well, I'll consider but I've got plans of my own," Abraham said, turning and preparing to sleep on a wadded-up flannel shirt.

"Plans? Good. There is no changing the world except by plans."

"I'm sleeping," Abraham said.

"You link your name to a great cause and then you'll sleep better. Plan that way and you can sleep for all time and people will remember you. Nobody will recall Denton Offutt, he was too much chasing after money, but, oh, that Abraham Lincoln, look what he did. Then, they might remember me after all."

"I'm sleeping," Abraham said.

"Starting out from Denton Offutt's store in New Salem, where he met and married Ann Rutledge."

Abraham resolved not to speak.

"Resolve a thing and it is half done," Offutt said. "You can make a promise to yourself inside yourself and then you've got your plan and you will see it through."

Abraham was sleeping, drifting back to his venture down river on the

173

little boat with Allen Gentry, crickets chirping, all tranquil, the embers of their campfire aglow, then yelling men, slaves with clubs coming, the biggest lug tossed into the campfire's coals, he shouts, panicking the others. Abraham wrests a club from one and begins flailing wildly, clipping one of the thugs on his head, who goes down, while the others back off into the night. Abraham was suddenly bleeding, aboard the old flatboat midstream, alone. Where was Allen? Abraham was anxious, he looked around, his heart pounding, breathing heavy as he scanned the waters. All at once Allen's face rose up from the waters, drowned but asking, laughing, "Did I scare you, Abe?"

Abraham woke up, eyes open, staring.

He was safe, nothing was happening, but he was weary.

He saw a star shooting and, looking about, Denton's silhouette.

After inhaling a long, deep breath, and feeling the boat rocking under him, Abraham fell back asleep.

CHAPTER SIXTY

The next morning, as Offutt was pissing out off the bow, he sang:

Awake, my soul, and with the sun
Thy daily course of duty run
Shake off dull sloth, and early rise.
To pay thy morning sacrifice.
Redeem thy misspent time that's past.
Live this day as if 't were thy last.

Hanks said, "If I were not so tired, I'd laugh."

"Hanks, you laugh, it'll do you good. Stop fretting. Time is wasting, you were never closer to death than this minute so you'd best wake up, shake a tail and live."

"I live," Hanks said.

"Ladies of New Orleans are Roman Catholic," Offutt said.

"Masses and saints and all?" Johnston asked. "Truly?"

"Oh, yes," Offutt said, and began to sing a raucous old frontier hymn:

There was a Romish lady, brought up in Popery—

"I see the city," Hanks said, interrupting and pointing, "church spires."

Offutt squinted.

"Time to laugh now, my boys. That right, Abe? Tell us one of your stories, lad. Last chance before there are ladies around and you won't dare to open your mouth."

"Well, the old Dutch farmer had a daughter..." Abraham began although attention was diverted from his merriment as they got more caught up in the horizon by the sound of wooden oar on wood, a throat-clearing sound, a compact series of increasingly higher notes. Nobody asked for a second story. The city was the chapter opening before them.

"It wasn't church spires, Hanks," Offutt said.

Hanks realized his error with awe at the same moment and opened his mouth, staring without blinking, saying one word, "Steamboats."

It was an awesome view. Nobody, neither Hanks nor Abraham on their previous trips, had seen half so many steamboats before. There had to be fifty vessels with smoke-stacks and side-wheels, often gaudily painted and carrying their names in huge black letters.

They were getting close now to the Gulf, close to New Orleans. The banks were all birds, warblers, robins, bluebirds, cardinals, grackles, sparrows, goldfinches, doves, pigeons, golden wing woodpeckers, redheaded woodpeckers, Carolina wrens and sparrow hawks. The fields were full of growing crops, promising a great harvest: corn, hay, rice, sugar, cotton, cotton, most of all, cotton. In one field, the harvest had apparently begun, two carts with huge all-wooden wheels being loaded with cut cane, teams of four oxen standing by to haul the load to be boiled down into sugar. Abraham wondered what he would do if he were one of the muscular slaves out in the cane fields issued a large, sharp knife.

"Lookee," Johnny said, the cabin boy of their *Santa Maria*, spying land ahead except that what we saw that caused him to shout was a pelican.

After the pelican, around the bend, came boats, at first only flatboats, moored and docked, probably over a hundred of them, all sizes, shapes and types, new and old, professionally-made and neatly-crafted, snug and trim, all the way down through the type of glorified raft with railings that Gentry and Abraham had, not knowing any better, felt was so grand until they docked in Saint Louis and, thereafter, humbly made their way to New Orleans. Then the steamboats, over fifty of them, likewise filling all categories on any such. And in the distance the tall-masted ocean-going vessels, the muscles of global commerce, in their sight. Abraham noted how different the port was, how much it had grown. There were at least three times the numbers from his trip three years before. It amazed him to speechlessness.

"Some of these boats may be from Cuba and Mexico," Abraham said. "All over."

"That's a lot of steamboats, John, you want to see?" Offutt called down.

"I got business," Johnny said, mucking the hog droppings. Life aboard the *Ark* went on notwithstanding its proximity to New Orleans.

CHAPTER SIXTY-ONE

Offutt and Abraham were up at the bow. Abraham was watching the waters ahead and plying the long oar slightly side to side. Offutt was standing, smoking a cigar.

They heard some noise, shouting from the stern room.

"What was that?" Offutt said, tensed as if to spring. He thought it might be fire. The room had a small brick cook-place, after all.

"It's Johnny, he's saying he's a man. He's late by two days. His birthday was yesterday and he reached twenty-one years the day before."

"That the law? A man the day before?" Offutt asked, puzzled no end.

Johnny came bursting out, leaping around atop the deck and shouting: "I'm a man!" I'm free, white and twenty-one! I'm a man today!"

"Happened days ago," Offutt yelled at him.

"Today's my birthday."

"Emancipated two days already and too ignorant to know it," Offutt said.

"That so, Abe?" Johnny asked.

"You were emancipated two days ago," Abraham said, continuing to scan the river. "But today you are as much a man as you will ever get."

Johnny ignored them as jokesters and worked himself up to shouting like a preacher at revival time, "John D. Johnston this day, on the river, reached his manhood. Today he can sign his own contracts now. He does not need no Pa. And Pa owns none of his earnings, not no more, no, sir."

With that Johnny was done and climbed down to the front to be with Abraham. Offutt offered a hand of congratulations. As Johnny and Offutt shook, Johnny asked Abraham, "It's true, ain't it? Pa has no more claim on my wages? You know the law, tell me, Abe. And don't fun."

"He owns your wages up until two days ago," Abraham said.

"But that's over now, it's all mine," Johnny said.

"Whatever you've earned under your minority, you owe him that, or Mr. Offutt here does. But the balance from here on is all yours."

"That don't seem fair," Johnny said, sulking.

"Pa put a roof over your head, he was responsible to clothe and feed you, get you an education or train you in work," Abraham said.

"He did as much for you and you get all your wages," Johnny said, almost crying from the sound of his whine.

"Pa won't keep it all, he always gave me something back. To keep me interested," Abraham said, thinking of how it was usually ten cents out of a dollar. "And he'll give you something to take away the sting."

"I feel like a slave," Johnny said, "honest I do."

"So don't we all," Abraham said. "The low rail of the fence will feel what it is if it has any sense, but at least you can rise in the world, John. Being a man and all. You make your own decisions from here on."

Johnny suddenly looked scared and appeared small, not as big as when he woke up shouting.

"I don't know what to do. I never had to decide before. I don't know what to do."

"Well, stick with us to New Orleans, at least," Abraham said, thinking of Sally and how kindly she was to him whenever he was scared. He had times when he felt like he was too small and too dumb to amount to anything. Abraham did not recall her words of comfort or any argument. Maybe there were no words. He just remembered how she made him feel. This feeling he recalled. He tried to make Johnny feel just as good now. He said, "Given a choice between staying on this boat and swimming, you got a decision but I figure you know what to do."

"I ain't swimming," Johnny said, laughing.

"You are the newest man among us so you've probably got the longest lifetime ahead, and the most decisions. Use your good head."

"I only got one head, Abe. That's the one I'll use."

"Start in New Orleans. See what they buy, what they sell, the difference in prices. Treat this here trip as free education."

"No, it ain't free. I'm paying," Offutt chimed in.

"My Pa gets the money, though. So you get my services free of any charge by me, the slave boy," Johnny said.

"You know nothing of slavery," Abraham said.

"Do, too."

"Do not."

"Do, so."

"You don't even know what day it is."

"My birthday."

"You mean May tenth?"

"Yes. May tenth."

"Today is May eleventh."

"Is not."

"Is, too."

Johnny looked to Offutt and asked, "Offutt, isn't it May tenth?"

"I don't know," Offutt said. "But your brother keeps track in an almanac."

"I keep track myself. It's May tenth."

"You must have slept through a day."

"Did not."

"Did, too."

"Bet you five dollars today's my birthday, May tenth."

Abraham held out his hand and Johnny gave it a vigorous shake.

They agreed to ask the date in the next town, Baton Rouge, to settle it.

"Enough now," Abraham said, not exactly raising his hand but putting it up toward the top of the long oar, with the fleeting illusion of a slap ready. He went on, "Be happy, Johnny. How many men before you died without ever seeing this city? Plus you'll have your own money."

"My own money. Those ten-dollar gold pieces," he said, then frowned, worried, thinking of Pa. "Did I earn them before or are they all mine?"

"Well," Abraham said, stroking his chin as if he had a beard and stringing out his words like a lawyer or a judge stating an opinion, "under terms of the agreement, which Pa signed, the gold pieces were not earned, due and payable until upon safe arrival at New Orleans. Thus, they accrues into your hands after age twenty-one and is entirely your own."

Johnny whooped and danced, sing-songing, "I got twenty dollars! I got twenty dollars! My own money in gold!"

CHAPTER SIXTY-TWO

The prior night they had anchored, it turned out, near a parliament of great horned owls engaged in a great debate. The novelty of the wisdom had gradually faded. Once, such an event had served as an exotic delight to all. Now, the hoots were so many torturous impediments to needed sleep. Abraham marveled how, after a time, the most astonishing marvels became irritations.

This night, because they were approaching the city of their destination, and because the weather was sultry and the air was so much sweat, everybody was nervous or excited or both and did not sleep. Instead of being in bunks or on watch, they paced, cat-like, on top of the flatboat. They strained to see lights downriver but only saw the blinking lights of craft moving at a distance, small as stars but not nearly as numerous.

"Care to talk?" Abraham asked Johnny.

"Huh?" Johnny asked, surprised.

"End of a long trip," Abraham said, somewhere between a statement and a question.

Johnny took it up by the question handle.

"It is, Abraham," Johnny said. "And not a wasted trip, a good trip. Pa will be pleased with us, won't he?"

"I think he will be."

"Pa trusted us. I mean, he could have kept me home or getting set to go back to Indiana."

"He had his reasons."

"He trusted us both, me, too. He let you go downriver before but not me."

"I remember."

"I remember, too."

"I remember you called me 'Horseface.'"

"Don't be angry."

"I'm not. You don't know me if you think I bear you any ill will, Johnny."

"Even if Pa, you know, favors me more than you?"

"Even so."

"Thanks, Abe."

Abraham said, "I'm a logical thinker."

"I'm glad, if that's what logical thinkers think."

"You find a cycle in human behavior, no progress, no good that lasts. Best be good to one another, that's all. Be good to one another."

"Isn't that what your Ma said before she died?"

Abraham was silent.

Johnny pressed no further.

As dawn approached, pairs of French mocking birds burst into song. Disturbed enough by their noises, Abraham thought of being a cat and pouncing on these noise-makers.

They got underway and could smell their approach to a dump-ditch manned by carrion crows and vultures who were either glutted from a surfeit of riches or were naturally lazy creatures, so much meat left out spoiling in the sun. They floated past a mysterious bar, unoccupied but covered with guano and feathers. Where were its settlers? Would they ever return?

They waved to cheerful wood-cutters, axes on their shoulders, walking to the next stand of trees that they would bring down. They were counted upon to clear land, and to create wealth from the stands they felled. Few occupations were more valuable and it was a way to make a living that Abraham was sure he would take up as soon as they got back to Saint Louis. No question but he could put his shoulder and upper body into the swing of an ax, and bring down the biggest, tallest trees with precise cuts made right. He had an eye for it and owed, he guessed, that much to his father.

Here, too, were geese, ducks and cranes, no swans seen, but the occasional bear sighting and the howls of distant wolves suggested that some of the slower birds might have gone without actually traveling anywhere. They heard the cry of the rare panther as well, the most chilling sound on a night that they ever wanted to hear. Anchored and safe, far from shore, they had a time returning to sleep nonetheless. They waited to hear some poor creature on the wrong end of an encounter with that cat-eyed, yowling, proud panther. Silence suggested an unsuccessful hunt. Perhaps he would practice stealth the next night. They were not going to be here to find out. As they approached the city, the leaping fish were so many and so evident that unlimited schools were indicated, ripe for any fishermen. Johnston and Hanks set out the willow poles and were not disappointed. Pretty palmetto plants lined many of the fences now. Fly-catching birds went about in their erratic, up-and-down madcap feeding flights. The moon was shining full and clear. As it must be back in Illinois, Abraham thought with a half-shock. Not everything was different, there was that connection with the moon.

He recalled and told the story of the slave who, when asked how far he thought it was to the moon, had answered his master, "Less than ten miles, I figure."

The master asked how the slave came to that conclusion.

"Well, massa," the slave said, "from atop the house I can just see them church spires on the way to Vicksburg that is ten miles away but can't be seen from hereabouts. But the moon? I can see the moon, so I figures it can't be but ten miles up there."

Offutt told the one about the balloonist forced down to a tree on a plantation as a slave was coming by.

The slave looked up and saw the balloonist in the tree and yelled, "Howdy, master Jesus, and how's your Pa?"

The waters of the Yazoo were clear and transparent, crystalline when Johnston thought it would be muddy with a name like Yazoo. Low willows and cottonwood on the banks made it seem a rich and verdant place worth stopping as a sight but they had a city to get to. The *Comet*, ten days out of Louisville, steamed past them to New Orleans, making a large wake that rocked their frail boat.

In another two days, they reached Baton Rouge.

CHAPTER SIXTY-THREE

At Baton Rouge, after they tied the *Ark* up at the pier and a watchman asserted that, for a fee in advance, their boat would be safe, Offutt paid the fee and ambled his way casually beside Hanks, Abraham and Johnny until he was approached by a short man in a worn coat and a wrinkled cravat. The two stepped aside and spoke briefly in whispers.

"Business, boys. Don't wait on supper for me, or worry if you don't see me until morning," Offutt said, waving, while Hanks, Abraham and Johnny wandered through town on their own.

They talked about Offutt. Hanks thought his "business" was a bordello while Abraham and Johnny thought "business" could mean just business.

"All night business?" Hanks asked in a doubtful tone.

"That's his business, I suppose," Abraham said.

They had spoken enough about Offutt.

The taverns here varied as to clientele. Some the tourists merely peeked in on briefly, then moved along, seeing frilly-shirted gentlemen, plantation-owners and men of business a class above them. They found two taverns to their liking. At the most crowded they stopped for a meal and water, figuring the crowd knew quality. In it, low-hatted, coarse-dressed, brogan- and boot-wearing boatmen and others who farmed nearby ate, drank and talked among dissolute inebriates and rowdy brawlers.

They had never seen the deft, shuffling hands of the experienced gamblers who set up at tables in several taverns along the town's single long street. Every so often, a chair at the card table would vacate and some new sucker stepped up to be fleeced.

"Do you see them handling cards?" Johnny asked, inclining his head toward a round table for six that was covered with banknotes and poker chips.

Because their little seven up card games had made them familiar with odds-defying and gambling tricks, and Johnny shuffled fairly well, he got an idea.

Hanks was unwilling, as was Abraham. Only Johnny wanted to stake something of his life savings upon the turn of a card.

Johnny said, "I can double this to something worthwhile. Most of these other players are drunk and will be fleeced and I am just the man to do the fleecing."

Johnny was feeling all of his twenty-one years. So far South, so old and so rich, it all went to his head.

185

"Go for it, then," Hanks said.

Abraham frowned but was not his brother's keeper.

As Johnny seated himself, smiling, Hanks said, "He don't have five dollars."

"And he won't have that in another two minutes," Abraham said.

"A boy's got to learn," Hanks said.

It was so. Johnny lost everything in a single game.

"Unlucky cards," Johnny said, shaking his head. "Who'd a thought?"

"If you only had another chance, the next hand you would of won," Hanks said, winking at Abraham.

"You bet, uncle," Johnny said, the irony of Hanks's remark over his head. "I had a feeling of exactly that."

They went to see other sights of Baton Rouge, such as they were. They passed fancy-dressed women who, whether old or young, looked hard. The fan-fluttering ladies spoke in high notes like birds, some in French, but none of the three replied to them at length. Even Johnny had gotten taciturn, knowing that he had no money.

They visited the market, noting how many customers were slaves with baskets and money.

"They don't run away," Johnny whispered to Abraham.

"You wouldn't run, either, if you were whipped or shot or hung for trying," Abraham whispered back.

They had had enough of Baton Rouge by then.

Back at the flatboat, Abraham cooked. He had bought a dozen eggs and several greens and made up a good scramble. A fresh loaf of bread and butter added to their dining pleasure. Filled, they went up atop the cabin. To their west a yellow-gold sunset was turning orange and purple. They watched, wordless, as the sun set, the horizon first kissing it and then swallowing it by inches, halfway, three-quarters, then but a sliver of light.

"It doesn't get any better than this, Abe," Hanks said.

Twilight. That old assault came suddenly flooding unbidden into Abraham's mind. The scar on his forehead gave a twinge. He watched the last splinter of sun sink below the horizon. By rights, he ought not be alive today. This stretch of river ought to have claimed him. Here, in the river, down a gator hole, ought to have been his last resting place. After a minute, Abraham spoke a few words as a sort of eulogy of their journey, as it was so nearly at an end.

He said, "A safe trip, nobody killed."

Hanks laughed, thinking that Abraham was just being funny.

CHAPTER SIXTY-FOUR

Early the next day, before dawn was even pink-fingered, Offutt came aboard yelling for everybody to get up and get going and launch. Abraham, on watch, easily attended to untying and setting the boat off, poling it back into the current, while Hanks and Johnny came forward, dressed but rubbing their eyes.

They found that Offutt had conducted some business while he was in Baton Rouge. At least, Offutt was able to divine that the main body of flatboats had passed through almost two weeks prior, at least ten days before. This was wonderful news. It meant that the peak glut on the market had come and gone and that prices were now rising.

"We'll sell those hogs for twenty cents, I guarantee," Offutt said in a shout.

"Hope so," and "good," Hanks, Abraham and Johnny said. Their fates and fortunes were now partly channeled through, up or down, the price of hogs in New Orleans. They were not in Illinois on the prairie any more.

The *Ark* was drifting swiftly now. The closer they came to the city, the faster the current. Greater care was needed for another reason as well: the *Ark* was not alone. Into their final miles on the river, two score flatboats, all larger than the *Ark*, and, today, a tooting steamboat were like so many horses racing toward the finish line. Recklessness prevailed not so much out of any necessity or economic incentive but from high spirits and a false sense of immunity from danger.

New Orleans was not in sight nor would it be for a few hours. Nonetheless, aboard the *Ark*, and aboard all of the rest of the river craft, the sense in the air was of a quest nearly realized. It excited them. Men yelled, cursed and hoorayed for the sake of sheer fun.

For lack of anything else to do or any other way to show his own excitement, Offutt took the stern pole and sent Johnny topside to give Hanks and Abraham a message.

Speaking to Hanks and ignoring Abraham, with whom he was surly, Johnny said, "Offutt says we'll be in New Orleans soon."

Abraham pointed over to the banks. They were within twenty yards of them.

"What?" Johnny asked.

"You see those plants?" Abraham asked Johnny.

"They look like green fans," Johnny said.

"Good guess. Fan palmetto. Indians eat the fruit. They live to be five hundred years old," Abraham said.

"You're fooling," Johnny said.

"You are looking at plants that were sprouts on that bank before Columbus," Abraham said.

"I'd rather look at New Orleans," Johnny said.

"New Orleans is coming soon enough," Abraham said. Hanks and Johnny were suddenly reminded that the only one of them who had been to New Orleans before was Abraham. He had noted that stretch of fan palmettos, apparently, three years before.

It was impossible. Johnny felt unable to keep silent.

"You use them as a marker?" Johnny asked Abraham.

"They point the way. And they will point the way after we're dust."

"How do you recognize them, and remember them?"

"How do you recognize or remember anything, Johnny?" Abraham asked. His tone was strange, as if he were at the threshold of a mystery too great for him, too.

It was peculiar that Abraham would speak so much with Johnny. Johnny wondered if it was on account of reference to death and to dust. Abraham, he had noticed, talked at greater length about death than about anything. He even had a poem he would recite about being in a graveyard. No matter, New Orleans was dead ahead. Ha.

"How long you think before we're there?" Johnny asked.

Abraham's eyes were entranced now, but he answered, saying, "We got to stop and anchor at dark. Got to, in this traffic. But if Offutt lets us haul up early, I reckon we could be there by mid-day."

Johnny shouted hooray and jumped in a quick jig. When he looked at Abraham, his brother was sober faced with no words. Johnny said, "Shucks, Abe, you seen New Orleans already."

Hanks was amused as the kittens fought.

He thought of something to tease Johnny with.

"For you, Johnny, New Orleans ain't going to be the only thing new," Hanks said.

Johnny said, "Don't be too sure it'll be all that new to me, cousin."

"Why? You found a gal this winter? Run the machine, did you?" Hanks asked.

Chasing a gal this past terrible winter was ludicrously comic to imagine. Of course, Johnny had done no such thing. Hanks — and now Abraham —

laughed to the point of braying at Johnny's facial expression. He looked like a cat who hit sour milk when he expected sweet.

"I ain't one to tell," Johnny said.

Hanks said, "Ain't you the randy one, now you got a beard?"

"I've had a beard a long time. I just let it grow this trip."

"You ain't answered my question," Hanks said.

Johnny shook his head, rose and disappeared down the scuttle-hole.

They both laughed again.

"You embarrassed the boy," Abraham said.

Hanks said. "He embarrasses himself. 'I've had a beard a long time.' He's a killer."

The two cousins from Illinois, one with a wife he missed and who missed him, and the other feeling alone in the world, remained atop the deckhouse, wordless again, watching as the stars come out. When Offutt said from the stern to weigh anchor and light the lamps, they did.

They would be in New Orleans the next day, probably not much after noon-time, at the very start of a busy afternoon.

But on land.

In the city.

And in the South.

ACKNOWLEDGMENTS AND FACTUAL REVIEW

Sources

This novel describes the journey of Abraham Lincoln to New Orleans with Denton Offutt, John Hanks and John D. Johnston. Lincoln said much more about his trip than he wrote about the Deep Snow winter that preceded it. Even so, it is not clear that anybody but Lincoln and his step brother made the entire trip. While it is certainly possible that all four men made the trip, as depicted in this novel, this fact is not documented consistently or clearly. It is possible that, for most of this trip, it was a two-man journey. Just as in 1828, when Lincoln at age 19 took a flatboat to New Orleans without other assistance than 17-year-old Allen Gentry, he may have been alone with John D. Johnston, his younger step-brother, in 1831. For example, Offutt may have traveled only to New Salem while John Hanks may have left at St. Louis for home (this latter scenario being exactly what Lincoln recalled, though not John Hanks, who recalled on the contrary that he went all the way to New Orleans).

Besides Lincoln's account of his trip, I drew heavily upon the papers of Lincoln's last law partner, William "Billy" Herndon. After his partner was assassinated, Herndon gathered contemporary accounts for use in a biography of his own making. What he gathered has been a controversial resource ever since. Herndon himself doubted the reliability of some of his informants while scholars have wondered about Herndon's own reliability. The waves of consensus disfavoring Herndon's papers swung more recently into favoring Herndon's intellectual integrity. I view Herndon as a man who pressed informants for details, even paying some of them handsomely for their help, making sacrifices to generate utterly irreplaceable documents of Lincoln's life from relatives, friends, business colleagues and even transient acquaintances.

(NOTE: Anyone visiting the Library of Congress and peering at microfilm copies will encounter many texts that are difficult, and in part impossible, to make out. To the great advantage of history, historical novelists, and people in general, Herndon's papers have been recently transcribed and expertly edited. Now published in a single annotated volume by editors Douglas L. Wilson and Rodney O. Davis, *Herndon's Informants,* (Chicago, University of Illinois Press, 1998)(hereafter, "HI"), Herndon's papers are dated, indexed, annotated and instantly accessible. Thanks to HI, I am able to direct readers to specific pages for my sources.)

Another source

Richard Campanella's thoroughly-researched, well-illustrated and beautifully-written *Lincoln in New Orleans, The 1828-1831 Flatboat Voyages and Their Place in History*, (Lafayette, LA, University of Louisiana at Lafayette Press, 2010)(hereafter, "Campanella") is unsurpassed on point of Lincoln's two trips downriver. I cannot overpraise Campanella's achievement.

John Hanks

Lincoln's favorite cousin, John Hanks, was an impressive and is an all-too-obscure figure in Lincoln's life. Through this novel, I am glad to make him better-known in this pivotal coming of age phase of the Lincoln we all know in history. Note that, but for Hanks's glowing report back to the Lincolns in Indiana, the family might not have trekked over 200 muddy, tree-blocked and rocky miles to Illinois. "Lincoln of Illinois" would have remained "Lincoln of Indiana," in that case, with unfathomable historical consequences.

As the cousin who introduced Lincoln to Denton Offutt and then accompanied Lincoln down the river, John Hanks, awaits full discovery and historical justice. His importance has not been recognized generally by historians and biographers. A gabby and less reliable cousin, Dennis Hanks, wrote so many colorful letters to Herndon that Dennis Hanks, rather than John Hanks, commands a spotlight in Lincoln studies. I am convinced that Lincoln was far closer to John Hanks, whom he not only liked but admired and followed.

Herndon went to Hanks for an interview only shortly after Lincoln's assassination. John Hanks gave a long statement to Herndon in 1865. Hanks's statement is a wonderful, fruitful gift to this day, one that invited me in particular to visualize the meeting between three members of the same family with a sort of trickster god who promised relief from their overwhelming troubles. It was from this encounter or interview that we know not only that Denton Offutt was an implacably dedicated mover and shaker operating in woodsy, wintry Illinois but also that Hanks himself recruited the impoverished and suffering Lincoln and Johnston for their potentially lucrative trip. Hanks told Herndon that *"Offutt Came to my house in Feb'y 1831, and wanted to hire me to run a flat boat for him — Saying that he had heard that I was quite a flat boatman in Ky: he wanted me to go badly. I went & saw Abe & Jno Johnson— Abes Step brother — introduced Offutt to them."* HI 456.

Hanks's later information on the canoe, the flatboat and the journey, provide many facts unavailable elsewhere that greatly supported reconstructing the trip in imagination. The novel reveals a factionalism or feuding on the flatboat, more dynamic interaction between Hanks and Offutt and between Lincoln and Johnston than Hanks's interview itself reveals or implies.

Lincoln and legal papers

Did Lincoln really draw up legal documents many years before he became a lawyer? Yes, indeed. As in volume one of this trilogy, *Deep Snow*, when Brown and Reed came by for an appraisal of a stray horse in December, 1830, the March 11, 1831 petition for a constable featured here is real. It was all in Lincoln's handwriting, signed by him and — in Lincoln's handwriting — ostensibly by John Hanks and John D. Johnston. The petition has been published and can be read in the *Collected Works*.[1] At I CW 3, the short but apt petition shows that Lincoln, while working on Congress land to chop wood, make lumber and build a flatboat, exuberantly performed a civic duty — for a county of which he was not then a resident and in which he had no self-interest or personal stake.

The flatboat

Lincoln, Hanks, Johnston and John Roll (and possibly several others, including Walter Carman, John Seaman, and one "Cabanis,") built a durable, if odd, flatboat which they launched and loaded. Lincoln, Hanks, Johnston and Offutt then cast off and floated down at least the Sangamon together — Offutt's speeches and activities are documented up to New Salem, and not much farther. They, or at least Lincoln and Johnston, drifted down other rivers to the Mississippi, then rode the Father of Rivers the entire distance to New Orleans. Historians agree that in their homemade flatboat constructed of "Congress land" (stolen) wood docked in New Orleans in about late May, 1831.

Hanks mentioned the flatboat's "plank sails" without more detail. Certainly, someone somehow thought of the idea of plank sails. Lincoln's lifelong interest in inventions (he is our only President with a patented invention) and mechanical things is well—documented elsewhere. See, e.g., HI From the fact that the flatboat they built had plank sails and the fact that Lincoln was avid about inventing it is a short leap to conclude that Abraham invented plank sails in 1831.

*

John Roll

Springfield area carpenter John Roll, ultimately a rich man and contractor who employed many hands, was a local who did help build a flatboat on the banks of the Sangamo River at Spring Creek, launching it in April, 1831. Lincoln later characterized Roll and himself as "slaves" at that time. Some have associated this with Lincoln's sense of injustice at a time that minor children were the *virtual* slaves of fathers who were entitled to all of their earnings. Nobody seems to have considered it instead a reference simply in the sense of impecunious laborers making a bare living, surviving on whatever coins or scraps or items in barter were tossed their way. As contract or hired labor for Offutt, Lincoln and Roll, both adult men, were at worst "wage slaves." That is, they "slaved away" or toiled for little remuneration.

Walter Carman and the canoe

Walter Carman and John Seaman (not Johnny Johnston) were, indeed, saved by Lincoln. That is, their canoe frolic into the raging spring flood is believed to be true. Although John Roll is this story's sole documented source, according to Roll, Sangamon County "inhabitants never tired of telling of the daring exploit." Abraham swiftly riding a log to rescue the two endangered men seems plausible and consistent with his character and quick thinking at other times. Campanella, p. 146.

The magician and Lincoln's hat

The magician and Lincoln's "low-crowned, broad-brimmed" hat (here imagined to have been black) is a true story. HI 373. Lincoln did act as cook, the group did play cards in their home-made shanty as they worked on the boat built out of (really) trees stolen from Federal land. The flatboat was somewhat as described in design and dimensions. See wonderful video/ reconstruction by Illinois

Ann Rutledge

Ann Rutledge may not have caught Lincoln's eye on April 19, 1831 during the night and day that the flatboat teetered disastrously on the lip of the Sangamon dam, but she probably turned out with others of the small village of over a hundred souls to see the excitement. Nobody has ever been more meticulous in tracing the primary documents behind the Lincoln-Rutledge romance than John Evangelist Walsh in his great but concise *The Shadows Rise, Abraham Lin-*

coln and Ann Rutledge (Urbana: University of Illinois Press, 2008). I am consistent with Walsh's conclusion that these two engaged in courtship and were looking to marry. I have, however, used my novelist's license both to advance, to accelerate and to intensify their interest in one another, probably earlier than they felt attraction — but *possibly* true to life, as love at first sight. (In Volume Three, Ann sends letters to Lincoln in New Orleans. No such correspondence is known, nor is it probable.)

Offutt's speech

Offutt did make a speech that sounded very much like the air-punching, grandiose address I composed for him to utter upon departing from New Salem in this novel. HI 254

Besides his speech, in this novel I have Offutt making deals. Deal-making is what Offutt did. All scholars agree that Offutt had an interest in the New Salem mill in late 1831, and a store, both of which Lincoln was assigned to manage, although I have found nobody else suggesting that his interests originated or unfolded during their change landing at New Salem and unloading cargo there due to an accident. Yet, which is the more plausible — that Offutt had plans and pre-existing contacts in New Salem, the very spot where the flatboat hit the dam, or that the accident led him to discover and to attempt to exploit the growing village's opportunities? (I concede that my theory of contacts-and-contracts in April requires Offutt's presence in April and that it is nowhere clearly documented that Offutt actually made the trip. Lincoln later said, somewhat ambiguously, that it was "during this boat enterprise" that Offutt concluded that he could "turn Lincoln to account" as a clerk in charge of a store and Mill at New Salem. One possible inference from that remark places Offutt aboard during the trip, if that is the meaning intended by the phrase "the boat enterprise.")

Hogs

For convenience, I combined the coarsely comic "eye-sewing" episode that did happen slightly later in their journey with the more dramatic rescue of the boat itself at New Salem. It is unquestionable that the crew sewed hogs' eyes. Lincoln himself, in his autobiographical sketch he wrote in 1860, verified the ludicrous "eye-sewing" event. However, it actually occurred just after they had relaunched off the dam and had made a few miles' progress down the river to one Squire Goodby's hog farm. IV CW 64.

*

The New Orleans mystery

A certain opacity arose around the end of the trip. In New Orleans *something* — something awful involving slaves — happened. Whatever it was seared Lincoln's conscience for life. At least one event involving slaves stung young man Lincoln so deeply that it reverberated later in American history.

What was it? We only have clues, clues from John Hanks's statements to Herndon. Bearing the fruit of emancipation, whatever happened took place in New Orleans then and was witnessed by 22-year-old Lincoln. As recorded over thirty years later, Hanks said of 1831 New Orleans:

> "There it was we saw Negroes Chained — maltreated — whipt & scourged. Lincoln Saw it — his heart bled — was thoughtful & abstracted — I Can say Knowingly that it was on this trip he formed his opinions of Slavery: it ran its iron in him then & there — May 1831." HI 457.

Now, scholars have identified contradictions between John Hanks's version and Lincoln's abbreviated account of the journey south — for example, Lincoln's version reports that Hanks left the flatboat in Saint Louis "for family reasons" and did not go the distance to New Orleans, 4 CW 64, while Hanks says that *"in May we landed in N. O."* HI 457. I reconcile Lincoln's and Hanks's conflicting reports in one way: Hanks heard so much from Lincoln that he took on Lincoln's memory as his own. New Orleans, 1831, was remembered and spoken of by Lincoln within his family but never publicly.

(Hanks seems to have admitted as much when he was sitting with Herndon. Herndon's surviving notes are a scrawled jumble that require close attention. Herndon's notes reveal that Hanks told him that Lincoln was *repeatedly vocal* about some searing slavery revelation or revelations in New Orleans. Herndon scrawled that Hanks said, *"I have heard him say [it]* — *often & often* — *Offutt* — *Johnson* — *Abe & myself left NO in June 1831."* This *"often and often"* reference to Lincoln's *conversation* is noted just *after* the remark that slavery *"ran its iron"* in Lincoln *"then & there."* Whether Hanks was present in New Orleans with Lincoln and at his side — as I depict in this novel — or Hanks heard Lincoln *"often and often"* talk about his New Orleans experience is not so clear. Lincoln was undeniably "front row center" at one or several instances of the maltreatment of chained or unbound slaves. Hanks is witness to *that*, to his cousin's lamentations and condemnation, if he was not a direct witness of the original "maltreatment" he summarized generally. Lincoln's reaction to, rejection of and resolve to fight slavery clearly dates from 1831.)

Lincoln's voices

Lincoln, who is recognized by a consensus of historians to have been superstitious, actually *did* hear voices in his youth. He once told his fellow lawyer, Henry C. Whitney, about the scariest of his Indiana days: *"I used to wander out in the woods all by myself. It had a fascination for me which had an element of fear in it — superstitious fear. I knew that I was not alone just as well as I know that you are here now. Still I could see nothing and no one, but I heard voices. Once I heard a voice right at my elbow — heard it distinctly and plainly. I turned around, expecting to see someone, of course. No one there, but the voice was there." Instead of replying directly to Whitney, who asked what the voice said, Lincoln displayed "(d)eep gloom —a look of pain — settled on his countenance and lasted some minutes."* Henry C. Whitney, "Lincoln a Fatalist," Rockport, Indiana, *Journal,* February 11,1898, quoted in Michael Burlingame, *Abraham Lincoln,* p. 24. I have developed that story into the articulation of "Blood coming." I think that the voice was likely to have brought Lincoln to worry about some fated, but vague, trouble. And, in Lincoln's case, few things were more troubling than blood.

Lincoln's own take on his travels

Lincoln himself looked back on this buoyant year of high hopes in a fond and affectionate mood. For our certainty about this, we may credit Charles B. Strozier. Professor Strozier elevated Lincoln's "autobiography," 4 CW 64, into prominence after its long obscurity. In it one may hear Lincoln's voice in the most lyrical section of his autobiography. An astonishingly disproportionate *one-quarter* of Lincoln's abbreviated autobiography (70 out of its 288 lines) is occupied by recounting those years, beginning with this short passage on the winter of the Deep Snow:

> *"During that winter, A. together with his step-mother's son, John D. Johnston, and John Hanks, yet residing in Macon county, hired themselves to one Denton Offutt, to take a flat boat from Beardstown, Illinois to New-Orleans; and for that purpose, were to join him — Offutt — at Springfield, Ills so soon as the snow should go off. When it did go off which was about the 1st of March 1831 — the county was so flooded, as to make traveling by land impracticable; to obviate which difficulty they purchased a large canoe and came down the Sangamon river in it. This is the time and the*

manner of A's first entrance into Sangamon County. They found Offutt at Springfield, but learned from him that he had failed in getting a boat at Beardstown. This led to their hiring themselves to him at $ 12 per month, each; and getting the timber out of the trees and building a boat at old Sangamon Town on the Sangamon river, seven miles N.W. of Springfield, which boat they took to New-Orleans, substantially upon the old contract. It was in connection with this boat that occurred the ludicrous incident of sewing up the hogs eyes. Offutt bought thirty odd large fat live hogs, but found difficulty in driving them from where he purchased them to the boat, and thereupon conceived the whim that he could sew up their eyes and drive them where he pleased. No sooner thought of than decided, he put his hands, including A. at the job, which they completed — all but the driving. In their blind condition they could not be driven out of the lot or field they were in. This expedient failing, they were tied and hauled on carts to the boat. It was near the Sangamon River, within what is now Menard county.

Lincoln also wrote:

"During this boat enterprise acquaintanceship with Offutt, who was previously an entire stranger, he conceived a liking for A. and believing he could turn him to account, he contracted with him to act as a clerk for him, on his return from New-Orleans, in charge of a store and Mill at New-Salem, then in Sangamon, now in Menard county..."

Hymns

The series of Baptist hymns that Offutt sings throughout this book are authentic, all drawn from a Baptist hymnal first printed in 1841, known as the "Primitive Hymnal." However, that hymnbook gathered many long-term favorites from prior decades. Although the pioneers of Illinois were not all Baptists (though Tom Lincoln was) most were Protestants and some familiarity with hymns was as endemic to social life as rock music among teen-agers from the mid-Twentieth Century on.

The river

Lincoln's paean to the river at pages 120-21 is drawn from a similar fragment that he wrote about Niagara Falls, II CW 10-11. His interest in nature and inventions (he later filed for a patent on a safety device for riverboats) was lifelong. He read books of science in preference to fiction or biographies, thinking most biographies to be false. A curious man, anything mechanical or moving he wanted to understand. I do not doubt that he journeyed down the Mississippi "all eyes" and senses, experiencing it. His senses were, thus, keen and at full intensity to receive what New Orleans offered, slaves and all. He was open to grasp and to understand and to deal with what he saw at age 22.

Summary

In summary:

> 1. dialogue and character's feelings or thoughts are reimagined as such elements are typically reimagined when real events are presented by historical novelists;
> 2. I aim for the possible when I cannot his the plausible or, even, the probable;
> 3. Overall, there was a trip downriver, an important event in Abraham Lincoln's life when he was 22 years old. This book's underlying structure is a foundation of actual facts and actual people of 1830–31.

NOTE: Except where I have imported some word or deed of Lincoln's from later in his life, no incident is presented that is knowingly inconsistent with the possibility of having occurred, nor does any character speak in a manner or about topics that are not contemporary. I strove to create a novel that is in keeping with Joseph Conrad's enduring definition of an author's task: to make the reader see. In fact, I hope to enable a reader to see, to hear, to smell, to feel and to taste this 1830–31 period of Lincoln's life. If a reader can experience this, he or she will know Abraham Lincoln that much better and, I think, be ever more in awe of him. He was never a "slave," and yet how far he had to climb. Before becoming the most beloved and skillful President we have ever had, Abraham Lincoln floated downriver with Hanks, Johnny and Denton Offutt, hung up on the New Salem dam, sewed hogs' eyes, and saw something searing in New Orleans that changed us all forever.

~~~

[1] Roy P. Basler, ed., *The Collected Works of Abraham Lincoln*, (New Brunswick, N.J.: Rutgers University Press, 1953), in seven volumes, (hereafter, "CW").

About the Author Print Edition

Wayne Soini's other historical novels include one about the Congressmen's duel of 1838, *The Duel,* (based on the duel between Jonathan Cilley of Maine and William Graves of Kentucky), *Nixon in Love* and *Germany Surrenders!* Before writing these novels, Soini wrote non-fiction, a local sports history with co-author Robert Fuchs, *Judge Fuchs and the Boston Braves,* (McFarland, 1998), *Gloucester's Sea Serpent* (Arcadia/History Press, 2010) and *Porter's Secret; Fitz John Porter's Monument Decoded,* (Peter Randall, 2011). Soini recently helped to research Charles B. Strozier's *Your Friend Forever, A. Lincoln* (Columbia University Press, 2016).

The Young Man Lincoln trilogy which starts with *Deep Snow*, continues in this book *High Water*, and concludes in the final volume, *Full Heart.*

Wayne Soini is a retired lawyer who holds a Master's degree in History from the University of Massachusetts Boston.

You can find the author on the web at: www.waynesoini.com

Join his mailing list to be notified of special discounts on new titles.

(His mailing list sign-up is: http://waynesoini.com/join-my-mailing-list/)

Made in United States
North Haven, CT
23 August 2022

23093521R00114